SHADOW DIRECTIVE

A DANNY CORTEZ THRILLER
BOOK 2

L.T. RYAN

WITH
ANDRE GONZALEZ

Copyright © 2026 by L.T. Ryan, Andre Gonzalez & Liquid Mind Media. All rights reserved. No part of this publication may be copied, reproduced in any format, by any means, electronic or otherwise, without prior consent from the copyright owner and publisher of this book. This is a work of fiction. All characters, names, places and events are the product of the author's imagination or used fictitiously. For information contact:

contact@ltryan.com

http://LTRyan.com

https://www.facebook.com/JackNobleBooks

For Devin.

Thank you for all the baseball bats you threw my way. The little toughness I have is because of you.

THE DANNY CORTEZ SERIES

Dead Man's List
Shadow Directive
Widow Protocol

CHAPTER ONE

WHILE DANNY CORTEZ watched the sun set over the Arizona desert, he pondered how many more times in his life he'd have to dodge death.

He had faced danger plenty—natural for how much time he'd spent hunting down lethal drug cartels operating within the United States. Three months had passed since he'd survived a shootout with the notorious drug lord known as Victor Villa.

Villa was back in prison, crippled and paralyzed from their last encounter in a bunker beneath a compound east of Las Cruces, New Mexico. The news reported Villa had returned to the supermax prison in Florence, Colorado last month after an eight-week recovery in the hospital.

Villa in a wheelchair for the rest of his life. The thought brought a smile to Danny's lips as he sipped a glass of lemonade.

"No more running from prison, Vic." Danny raised his glass to the sunset casting a purple and orange glow over the town of Jerome, Arizona.

After confirming Villa's cartel, Los Leones, had been disbanded—many fled, but others were captured and awaited trial—Danny had sought the return of his mother to the retirement home she'd adored in Colorado.

Nadia protested the decision after all the work she had done to help move Tatiana out east. His mother had some initial confusion about moving back so soon, but Danny had convinced both women it was for the best with the cartel no longer a viable threat.

After getting her settled, Danny ventured back to the desert in search of a quiet town where he could relax and rehab the ankle Villa had put a bullet through. He'd gone through surgery to repair a torn ligament, and he would forever lack a few shards of bone, but the doctor assured him of a full recovery.

Within the last month, Danny had regained his ability to walk without pain and had begun light jogging in the early mornings before the temperature climbed toward one hundred and twenty degrees in the scorching afternoons.

Danny hated being stuck inside during the day, but the doctor ordered extensive rest for the ankle to heal faster. He hunkered down in a nine hundred-square-foot studio apartment two blocks from Main Street.

Having little to do, Danny had dived back into his old passion for books. He read nearly six hours each day, sometimes more. He struggled to find anything worth watching on TV, so books and music had become his comfort food. He'd kept to himself and hadn't befriended any locals, except for a blind man who worked at the small library in town.

Without an escape, dark thoughts flooded Danny's frantic mind. His mother, who suffered from dementia came first. Then Nadia, his version of the one who got away, and who still stayed in touch to help Danny out of sticky situations. And finally, his friend and former colleague in the DEA, Zak, who'd risked it all to save Danny from certain death at the compound hidden in the New Mexican desert.

Danny drew in a deep breath and finished his lemonade. The soothing sounds of Santana strumming a guitar spilled from the mini speaker sitting on his patio table. It had become routine for Danny to watch the sunsets. The ritual soothed him, bringing an inner peace he hadn't experienced in years. Yet, no matter how peaceful life appeared, he understood the truth of the world.

He dropped off his empty glass in the kitchen sink and scooped up his cell phone from the countertop. His mother usually called him before she went to sleep for the night, but she hadn't reached out yet. He'd wait another hour before calling her himself.

Danny slipped his phone into his shorts pocket and raised up on his tiptoes, lowering and raising every ten seconds. The doctor suggested this simple exercise to help restore the strength of his ankle and surrounding muscles. A month ago, he could only do three reps before his ankle gave out and demanded he quit. Today, he did forty and would strive to add one rep each day until he could easily do one hundred.

His phone buzzed in his pocket, and he snatched it, ready to answer the call from his mother.

Only it wasn't a call. Nor was it his mother.

The screen showed a preview of a text message from an unknown, restricted phone number. His stomach churned. Nothing good had ever come from someone hiding behind the other end of a text message.

Danny opened the text message and found a list of names:

Marcus Vance

Eva Ramirez

Amber Williamson

Zakary Larocque

Aaron Murphy

"Marcus Vance?" he asked himself.

Vance rattled a memory, but Danny struggled to pinpoint it. He studied each name. Zakary Larocque was his friend Zak, the only man who could be trusted within the DEA nowadays.

That's when the connection hit him. Marcus Vance had been one of several instructors Danny had in his early days of training at the DEA. Did the other names have similar connections to the DEA?

Who is this?

But he hesitated to hit send. If he did, then it would all start again. The mind games. The puzzles and vague clues. He was no stranger to this. Barely three months removed, in fact. There were still loose ends from the debacle with Victor Villa and Los Leones. Loose ends he never followed up on because he wanted nothing more than to get the hell out of town and be done with it.

How did that saying go? Set something free, and if it's meant to be, it will come back? What a crock.

But here it was, sitting on his virtual doorstep. Villa was locked up, his cartel vanished, but another player had laid their cards down. One who never identified themselves. One who had pulled strings for both Villa and Danny, like a twisted dog owner forcing his pets to fight each other to the death.

We're all just pawns in someone else's life. Some of us never realize it. Never meet the puppet master hiding behind the curtain. And some of us have the horrifying moment of clarity when it all comes crashing down.

He pressed send and watched his message go out to its unknown recipient. There were still corrupt people working in the DEA. All the focus had been on Villa, and the Justice Department had no reason to look elsewhere after the old man had been thrown back into prison.

And that's all my fault.

All Danny had to do was tell someone. Anyone outside of the DEA. Nadia was the first to come up in his mind. She had been the last time, too, and she'd ended up kidnapped. They'd already had eyes on his mother, who was supposed to be hidden away in a remote location. Which left Zak as his only trustworthy insider, but neither Danny nor Zak could risk Zak losing his job.

It had taken time, but they'd found him. When you carried deadly secrets, those who didn't want those secrets released would stop at nothing to hunt you down.

Danny hadn't thought once about packing his lone suitcase since he'd arrived in Jerome, but now he scanned the studio, calculating how long it would take to pack up everything and leave.

Twenty minutes max. He always traveled light. Just in case.

His preparedness made his life boring, predictable. But it kept him alive.

When his phone buzzed with a response, staying alive was all he cared about.

Danny opened the text message and grabbed his Glock 17 from the kitchen drawer. Once again, the message wasn't clear, but the three words were plenty to make him concerned for his safety.

Choose a side.

CHAPTER TWO

AFTER A NIGHT OF RESTLESS SLEEP, Danny rolled out of bed at five o'clock the next morning. He brewed a cup of coffee from the whiny machine he'd picked up at a thrift store, put on his jogging shorts, and went for his morning run.

Despite the thermostat reading a tick below seventy degrees, the morning air was cool against Danny's skin as he jogged through the neighborhood.

His ankle progressed with each passing day, and last night's text message added extra fuel to his motivation to get back to full strength. A fight loomed. With whom, he didn't know. But the day would come soon enough. He ran harder than he could remember during the last two weeks, pushing himself into a drenching sweat by the time he returned to his apartment thirty minutes later.

Aside from his recovering ankle, Danny appreciated that the rest of his body was in pristine shape. Perhaps the strongest it had ever been. No lingering pains in his knees or back. No hamstrings on the verge of snapping under pressure. The extended rest had cured his entire body, making him feel brand new.

Danny returned and took a quick, cold shower before dressing for the day. It was only six o'clock now, the sun barely above the horizon, when he grabbed his cell phone and debated making a call that had troubled him all night.

Chicago was two hours ahead, so he dialed Nadia. *She's not going to answer. Why would she?*

The last time they spoke, she had requested he stop contacting her unless it was regarding his mother. Danny hoped the passage of time had softened Nadia's disgust toward him. She and Zak were the only people Danny had shared his concerns with about the DEA being overrun by corruption. Zak obviously had his suspicions working in the D.C. office but had uncovered no evidence of wrongdoing.

His heart hammered as the phone rang.

"Hello, Danny." She sounded as enthusiastic as a janitor getting ready to scrub a toilet.

"Nadia!" His voice elevated to a pitch he hadn't intended. Danny cleared his throat and brought it down a notch. "Thanks for answering."

"I didn't want to. But you've done a good job respecting my wishes so far. Is something wrong with your mother?"

Even in her condescending tone, Danny couldn't help but feel a spark when hearing her voice. A hopeless romantic, he believed one day they would find their way back to each other. The only time he'd forgotten about Nadia, romantically, was during his time with Sofia Hernandez in New Mexico. But like most other women in Danny's life, she had vanished as quickly and unexpectedly as she'd arrived.

"That's not what I'm calling about," he said. "But now that you mention it, she never called me last night. And she didn't answer when I tried. I'm not worried about that, though—that's happened a couple of times."

Nadia softened her tone. "Dementia only gets worse, Danny. Never better, I'm sorry to say."

"I know. I'm gonna drive out to visit her. Either today or tomorrow."

"Where are you even staying these days?"

"About thirty minutes outside of Sedona."

"Arizona? In June? You must be out of your mind."

Danny chuckled. "It's not terrible if you run all your errands before nine a.m."

"What's going on, Danny? I just got into the office a few minutes ago and have to prepare for court."

"I'm not entirely sure, but there's a situation. I received a text message."

Danny paused, unsure of who exactly to accuse of sending it.

"And?" Nadia replied, her impatience growing. "I get at least five text messages every hour. What's your point?"

"I think it's from someone involved with the Villa matter. Well, someone from the DEA."

Nadia sighed. "You're still on that?"

"I'm not making this up."

"Danny, I don't know how many times we need to have this discussion. I have plenty of contacts in the DOJ. Ones I'd trust with my life. They've all confirmed nothing is going on with the DEA. Yes, lots of people don't like Chuck Steele for the way he runs the department, but no one is accusing him of corruption."

"These guys are smart. They know their way around the government. They're not going to make it a simple task to catch them."

"Humor me, Danny. What did the text message say?"

Danny put the call on speaker and navigated to the message to read it verbatim. After listing the names and the closing message, he said, "It's not from the cartel—they're gone. Leaderless. Who else would have a list of DEA agents, besides the DEA themselves? And *choose a side*. What the hell is that supposed to mean? There are no sides. Unless there's a new cartel, but that seems unlikely right now."

Nadia remained silent. Danny heard only the ruffling of papers in the background.

"You can't explain it, can you?" Danny pressed on.

"What do you want from me, Danny? I'm tired of getting sucked into your drama."

"Don't you get it? You're still in it. The same people who kidnapped you are still out there. That wasn't the cartel. And if they did it once, they can do it again."

"Yes, I'm aware of that. But what reason do they have to even talk to me again? Everything that happened was them forcing you into catching Villa. Which again, I don't think it's the DEA. They have the resources to catch any criminal they want. No need to involve you."

Danny's laugh was devoid of any humor. "So you're still stuck on this mysterious third-party theory. Like there's a shadow agency pulling the strings."

Nadia almost growled, and Danny could imagine the way her nostrils would flare. "I don't know, Danny. It makes more sense than the DEA. The only corruption I'd expect from the DEA is them keeping and selling drugs or taking the money they find at drug busts. Not blackmailing an ex-agent into capturing an escaped convict. I have a problem with things that don't make sense. And everything you're saying doesn't make sense for the DEA."

"Fine. Agree to disagree. Regardless of *who* it is, the fact remains we're both still in danger."

"Do whatever you need, Danny. But I will not be dragged into this again. I have my own battles to fight every day in the courtroom. I don't need yours on top of it. Are we clear?"

Danny gulped. "Clear."

"Good. This is the last I want to hear about any of this. Have a good day."

Nadia hung up without letting Danny respond.

I love you, Nadia.

Not a day passed that he didn't beat himself up for leaving a life with Nadia behind. He could have been spending his days at a basic desk job in Chicago, coming home to cater to his attorney wife, and making love to the most incredible woman he'd ever known.

Instead, he'd chosen this path, bouncing from small town to small town, just trying to stay alive.

Hindsight, right?

One thing Danny hadn't lost throughout his troubled life was his intuition. His gut guided him everywhere he went. And today was no different.

Something terrible awaited in the coming days, and every alarm in his mind and body blared to alert him. If they had found the number for his latest burner phone, how long would it be until they pinpointed his location? Then his nightmares would come true.

Danny didn't need to leave Jerome, but his instincts demanded he visit his mother in Colorado. Maybe it wasn't even for her own safety, but his own need to say goodbye. As he'd done so often. As her mind regressed, Danny wasn't sure how many of his goodbyes she even recalled. Always worried about his potential last day on Earth, he'd lost count of how many times he wished his mother farewell—for what he believed was the ultimate time.

And each time he had, he'd survived. Maybe it was all part of the ritual. Whether fate or coincidence, Danny was just superstitious enough not to change his routine.

He rummaged through his clean clothes and filled a duffel bag with enough for a week-long visit to Colorado. Hopefully, it would pass seamlessly, and he could return to Jerome and the slice of peace he'd found.

He drew the curtains, unplugged everything from the outlets, and loaded the dirty dishes from the sink into the dishwasher. Checking the fridge, he found his jug of lemonade nearly at its end. Danny poured a short glass and finished it, drawing in a deep breath as he looked around the studio for any last things he forgot to pack.

Once satisfied, Danny slung the duffel bag over his shoulder and headed for his Tundra parked outside. The drive from Jerome to Aspen was ten hours. He fired up the engine with one thought keeping him motivated.

I get to have dinner with my mom tonight.

CHAPTER THREE

DURING THE DRIVE, Danny's mind bounced from one topic to the next as he flew down the freeways in the middle of nowhere. He thought about the past. The future. His life wasn't exactly in shambles, but it wasn't where he wanted it to be, either.

His main problem was not knowing exactly what he sought. Settling down only seemed right if it could be with Nadia. For now, that was a long shot. His odds of meeting someone else were even less, considering how little time he spent in each location he visited. Sofia had been that rare exception during his time in New Mexico, but she'd made it plenty clear she never wanted to see him again.

Driving through the Rockies, however, made him long for home. Always having someone after him, threatening his life, Danny refused to stay anywhere near his hometown of Denver. He didn't need any criminals knowing where his mother lived, or the location of his childhood home, now sitting empty on the west side of Denver.

If he could eliminate whoever had sent him those odd text messages, maybe he could trust the universe enough to move back into his old house. But he doubted any of that would hold true. Trouble always followed him.

He had enjoyed living in D.C. If matters cleared up and the corruption got rooted out, maybe he'd take another crack at working for the DEA. He'd only left because of the psychological toll from losing his partner. But he'd made peace with that chapter of his life during the past few months.

Danny entered Aspen shortly after five o'clock and parked at the Morning Star Retirement Community by 5:25, climbed out of the truck, and stretched. His lower back ached after sitting for such an extended time, having only stopped once in Utah to fill up with gas and grab lunch, but the crisp mountain air filled his lungs and made everything better.

Maybe I should live here in Aspen.

He had the money, but could he really live among so many rich assholes? These people put on gaudy jewelry and makeup just to buy a gallon of milk from the grocery store. How could he expect to go anywhere in town and fight off the urge to choke all the entitled idiots?

Aspen was out, but there were plenty of small mountain towns he could disappear into. Communities where everyone kept to themselves and yet still looked out for each other.

Danny cracked his neck and started for the entrance, whistling a Sinatra tune under his breath. A couple of workers sat on the bench outside, enjoying cigarettes on their break. Aspen had perfect summer weather, and he couldn't blame them for enjoying it.

He passed through the automatic sliding doors and entered the lobby. A plump woman sat behind the reception desk, cradling a phone between her shoulder and ear, typing on a keyboard.

She hung up as Danny approached. "Mr. Cortez?"

Danny had met and spoken with so many people from the home, it was impossible to remember. The woman sounded familiar, but he couldn't pinpoint a name until seeing it on the badge clipped to her shirt.

April.

"Yes," Danny said, leaning against the desk. "I just need a visitor's pass to visit my mom. Tatiana Cortez."

They had used aliases during his mother's previous stay in the home. But with the cartel out of the picture, Danny felt comfortable enough to use her legal name. Plus, it reduced the confusion she already had to endure thanks to the escalating dementia.

April frowned as she clicked around on her computer. "Give me a moment, Mr. Cortez. I'll be right back."

She rose from her creaky chair and vanished down the nearest hallway, leaving Danny alone to strum his fingers on the desk as he waited. He glanced around and spotted a group of the residents playing cards in the community room. A handful sat in front of a TV watching Jeopardy.

April returned three minutes later with a man in a suit. Danny recognized him as Albert Legumina, the director of Morning Star.

Albert approached with a stern expression and stuck out his hand while April circled her desk to sit back down. "Good to see you, Mr. Cortez. Did you forget something here?"

"Uh…no. I'm here to visit my mother." Danny furrowed his brow and shook the man's hand, paranoia getting the best of him—a symptom of having endured constant terror at some point or another for the past several years. "What's with all the added security? Am I not allowed here?"

Albert licked his lips. "Mr. Cortez, she's not here anymore. You authorized her transfer just two days ago. Forgive me for not understanding your confusion."

Danny's gut twisted into knots, the slightest tremble creeping into his arms. "I never authorized anything."

Albert drew in a deep, panicked breath. His eyes darted around the lobby as if a logical answer might pop out of a cabinet drawer. "Mr. Cortez, I personally spoke with you on the phone two days ago regarding this matter. You called in to authorize a crew of relatives to help move your mother out. You provided the correct passcode. It was you on the phone. I had no reason to doubt it."

But doubt had already infiltrated Albert's voice.

Danny scratched his temples with both hands. It suddenly felt like he was back in Arizona. The lobby had to be over 100 degrees.

"I never called," he said. "I just drove here from Arizona to visit my mom, and now you're telling me she's not here. One of us is living an alternate reality, and it's not me."

"We had a farewell party for her last night, and she left with the group of people you said would be here. Relatives. Tatiana chatted with them right away. Seemed like she knew them." Albert's eyes danced all over the room, searching for a better explanation. But failing. "Everything seemed so normal. You've always lived out of town, and we thought nothing of you making the request to move her out over the phone—that's why we have the passcodes."

"Take me to her room." Danny wasn't sure if he was close to crying, screaming, or ripping someone's head off.

"There's nothing—"

"Take me to her room."

Danny gritted his teeth so hard it was a miracle none popped out.

"Certainly. Follow me." Albert pivoted and started down the hallway.

Danny's legs turned to Jell-O as he followed the suit, passing six different suites on his way to the end of the hall, where his mother should have been.

The "T. Cortez" nameplate no longer hung on the wall. When Danny stepped into the room, every ounce of blood froze in his veins.

A stripped-down bed stood in the middle of the room. The nightstand next to it had nothing on it. The walls, once covered with old family pictures, were bare. A tall dresser, normally with clothes bursting out from the drawers, stood cleared out.

Danny approached the bed and brushed a finger along the bare mattress. "Where the hell is my mother?"

Adrenaline flooded his body. The trembling in his arms grew into an uncontrollable shake of each limb.

"Mr. Cortez, she's gone. I'm not sure what's going on, but we did everything you asked us on the phone."

"I NEVER CALLED HERE!" Danny screamed.

He grabbed beneath the bed frame and flipped it completely over with a resounding crash. Someone gasped from the hallway and hurried footsteps rushed to the open door.

Albert spoke in a composed tone to whoever checked on the room. "Everything's fine. Go."

"I never called here," Danny repeated, seething. "I had no intention of moving my mom out of here. She and I agreed she would spend her final days in this facility. She loved it here. Who did you speak with on the phone?"

Danny spun around, rage filling his eyes, which narrowed on Albert. The poor man turned pale as a ghost. He didn't fight the rage that took over his voice? "Who did you speak with?"

"I—I thought it was you. The man said his name was Danny Cortez. And he gave the passcode. Armando724."

Danny's middle name—his father's first name—plus Danny's birthday of July twenty-fourth.

"This is a kidnapping," Danny said. He fought the urge to shove Albert into a corner and demand answers. But that would get him nowhere except for maybe an escort to the parking lot. "We don't have time to waste. I never called here. Didn't authorize anyone to take my mom. How many people were there?"

"Four. They said they were all family. They greeted Tatiana with hugs and kisses. Like I said, she knew them."

"She can barely remember her own name!" Danny snarled. He balled his hands into fists.

If he hadn't come today, how long would it have been before he learned his mother had been taken from her home?

"Do you want me to call the police, Mr. Cortez?"

"I don't need the police," Danny said. "I know this place has security cameras all over. Give me the footage showing who all was here last night, and I'll take it from there."

Albert gazed at Danny, stuttering unformed words.

"NOW!" Danny shouted.

Albert nodded, sweat trickling down his forehead. "Yes. Yes. I can do that. Wait right here."

He ran out of the room, leaving Danny alone.

When he drew in a deep breath, Danny could still smell his mother's lingering scent. The smell of home.

Danny flipped the bed back over and sat on the edge, already plotting his next moves.

"Whoever did this …" he said to himself, "they're dead."

CHAPTER FOUR

DANNY WASTED no time after watching the footage.

Albert was gracious enough to connect Danny with the head of security, who pulled up the recording of a group of four people who had entered Morning Star yesterday evening. They zoomed in on their faces, and Danny didn't recognize any of them.

Three men and a woman.

They were all of Latin descent. Professionals. They would have infiltrated the retirement home's system to learn Danny's passcode to forge the phone call authorizing his mother's release.

The ease with which they strolled into the home and interacted with the staff and his mom made him queasy. They were confident. Trusted they wouldn't get caught. The woman talked with Tatiana while the three men packed up her belongings and hauled boxes out.

The footage followed them to the parking lot—after the farewell cake Morning Star had provided to toast Tatiana—where they tossed the boxes into the rear of a black Cadillac Escalade. They helped Tatiana into the passenger-side back seat and stowed her wheelchair in the back with the rest of her belongings.

On camera, the kidnappers showed her care and respect. But what had they done since driving off at 7:18 p.m.? Over twenty hours had passed since they'd left Morning Star with her. Plenty of time to drive just about anywhere within the continental United States.

The security team downloaded the footage and gave it to Danny on a flash drive. He returned to his truck, nauseated. Were they giving her the meds she needed to control her dementia symptoms? Were they feeding her? Helping her use the restroom?

The thought of his mother helpless with those goons blasted a fire through Danny's veins. Killing was the only thing on his mind, but that wouldn't help locate her. He needed composure and a plan, both of which appeared out of reach.

The SUV had no license plates. Danny begged Albert not to involve the police, but understood it was only a matter of time before he would. Albert had to cover for his business, after all. And having an elderly dementia patient kidnapped right in front of his eyes would surely spell doom.

Maybe he won't get the police involved. That will only lead to press coverage and questions he has no answers to.

It didn't matter to Danny as he sat in the Morning Star parking lot, squeezing the flash drive, and dialing his phone with the other hand. It was nine o'clock on the east coast, and Danny expected his friend to answer.

"Hello?" the voice said from over two thousand miles away.

"Zak. It's Danny. Is it safe to talk?"

Zak replied in a hushed tone, "Can I call you back on this same number?"

"Not a problem."

"Give me one minute."

The call disconnected. Danny stared at his phone. Forty seconds later, it rang from a different number.

"Zak? Everything okay?"

"It is now," his friend said. "Rather be safe than sorry. Got a burner phone just for calls with you."

"Still that bad at the office?"

"For some of us. Steele has remained secretive about the cases he's overlooking. Sends out random assignments to the agents. I think I'm on his good side, but he still isn't letting me in. I'm handling all the duties of the deputy director without the title. Or the pay. Enough about me. Why are you calling so late?"

"Something terrible has happened. I'm glad we're on a secure line because I'm still convinced someone at the DEA is involved. And by the sounds of it, it's got to be someone working with Steele."

"He acts like he has plenty to hide. What happened, Danny?"

"They kidnapped my mom. Took her right from her retirement home after posing as me during a phone call to authorize her release. They came in, packed her things, and left with her in an SUV."

Saying this aloud to Zak made tears rush to Danny's eyes, the urge to cry suffocating him.

"They did *what*?!"

"There's more. They texted me before any of this happened—well, it would have been *while* this was all happening. But they didn't mention my mom. They listed names and told me to choose a side."

"What names?"

"Your name is on the list." Danny told him the series of names he'd memorized.

"These are all DEA agents," Zak said. "Or ex-agents. Not sure what I have in common with any of them, but I recognize them. I'll dig in and see what I can find. What can I do to help find your mom?"

"I'm not sure right now. They called into the retirement home from a blocked number. The security guy thinks he can get the phone company to reveal the number, but there are no guarantees. Could take time to get that information. All we could tell from the video footage was they headed east from the home. But that doesn't give us much to work with."

"No plates?"

"Nope."

"I'm gonna need some time, Dan. It's too risky for me to look into this at the office. We have regular audits, and I'm sure Steele keeps a close eye on everyone working in that building. They've uploaded all kinds of spyware on our computers."

"How are you supposed to do anything?" Danny asked.

"The old school way. Talking to people I know. Afraid I won't be able to find much on your mom, but I can ask around about the names on that list. Just to see what people have to say."

"And you're sure you can trust these people?"

"Of course. Steele may have purged people from the DEA, but there's still plenty of us on the right side."

"Be extra careful. You're on this list, and I don't know what it means."

"I agree. We also need to keep our communication to a minimum. Save this number for my burner phone. Don't call me during the day. Wouldn't be surprised if Steele set up wires around the office to listen to our conversations." Zak cleared his throat. "Think you can make it out to D.C. anytime soon? Would be beneficial for us to discuss this in person."

"I'll see what I can do," Danny said. "Need to know how closely I'm being watched first. No idea how they found me in Arizona, but if they know I'm in Colorado now, I can't risk going to you."

"Think Nadia would serve as a middleman for us? She can relay our messages to each other. Might cut out some of the suspicion."

"I doubt it. She's not too thrilled with me these days. Plus, she's made it plenty clear she doesn't want to be dragged into any drama I'm involved in."

Zak groaned, but kept his tone cool. "Okay, that's fair. We'll figure something out. For now, just make sure not to call my regular number. Give me a few days and I'll see what I can learn about those names. Hopefully, I can find a link that will reveal who is behind all of this."

Danny rubbed his forehead. "Do you think anyone there has anything to gain from kidnapping my mother?"

"It's definitely drastic," Zak said. "I doubt even Steele would attempt such a vicious act, but he is a loose cannon. Let's not jump to conclusions. Hang tight, and don't get yourself into trouble."

"Thanks, Zak. I'm gonna find a hotel out here in Aspen and make a plan for the coming days."

They hung up.

No answers about my mom. And now Zak is likely in danger.

Danny punched his steering wheel repeatedly until his knuckles turned raw.

How am I supposed to plan if I don't even know which way they went?

Danny fired up his engine and sped out of the parking lot to head back into town. Anytime he spotted a black SUV, he trailed it until he confirmed his mother wasn't inside. He had followed three before the reality set in that maybe he was being irrational.

But how couldn't he be?

He kept his Glock under the driver's seat, ready to blast at anyone who tempted him. As much as he fantasized about shooting at his mother's kidnappers, he wouldn't risk her life. Any decisions required calculation. An emotional reaction would only cause unnecessary death.

It wasn't until twenty minutes later, after checking into a somewhat reasonable hotel for the low cost of two hundred and fifty dollars a night, that he unraveled entirely.

Aspen. What a rip off.

Within thirty minutes of settling into his room, Danny emptied the mini-bar into his stomach. After tossing back the eight different shots —yes, he understood mixing alcohols would cost him in the morning he grabbed a pre-rolled joint from his duffel bag and locked himself in the bathroom. He ran the shower until steam filled the room and sealed off the bottom of the door with a towel.

The marijuana smoke had never felt so necessary as his anxiety spiked to new levels. Danny may as well have been a caged bird, useless to the world outside his prison of worry.

For the first time in his life, Danny Cortez had no idea what to do.

CHAPTER FIVE

DANNY WOKE the next morning with a rational mind after a night of deep sleep.

The joint had done its job. Sleep would have otherwise been impossible. His paranoia after smoking had spiked, knowing his mother was out there with dangerous thugs. But the THC soon knocked him out cold. Plus, it left him with only a mild hangover after the mini-bar shots.

They can't hurt her. They took her for leverage over me. Hurting her only weakens whatever they're trying to use me for.

He woke up with these thoughts as his only reassurance.

When he rolled out of bed and picked up his phone from the hotel room's desk, he discovered twelve missed calls from Nadia, all of which had come through within the last hour.

A call every five minutes? His stomach dropped to his knees. Nadia never made such desperate attempts to get hold of him.

Danny called her back and paced the room while waiting for her to answer.

"Danny?" she answered, her voice in a panic. "Where the hell have you been?"

"Nadia, what's wrong? I'm at a hotel in Aspen. My mother's been—"

"I know about your mom." She lowered her voice to a near whisper. "It's them, Danny. Whoever kidnapped me last time."

He sat at the foot of the bed, lightheaded with his stomach grumbling. "How do you know that?"

"I don't have any proof," she said. "I just *feel* it. Got a strange text message last night. Saying I need to force you to comply. I ignored it, thinking it was a hoax. But they kept texting. All the messages were about you. How your loyalty was critical to the bigger picture." Nadia paused and sniffled. Was she crying? "Danny, what is going on?"

Danny clenched the cell phone and gritted his teeth. This was not how today was supposed to begin. "We're all in danger. These guys kidnapped her last night and I would've never known if I hadn't come to visit. No idea where they took her."

"Let me guess, you haven't called the police?"

"Of course not. That will bring publicity and cause a scene. People like this operate in the dark. They only took my mom to negotiate with me. If the cops get involved, I lose bargaining power. If they see no value in keeping my mom safe, I don't want to think about what they'd do to her."

Nadia's voice quivered with each of her next words. "What have you done, Danny?"

Danny scoffed. "Are you implying this is my fault? I've been keeping to myself in Arizona. My mom was safe in her home. This was all supposed to be over with Villa out of the picture."

"Well, it's not. I suppose you're going to rescue your mother on your own?"

"Of course not. I'm going to need help. You. Zak. Anyone else we can trust?"

"Danny, I can't just leave my job again and chase down some secret shadow agency. I'm expected to appear in court. Judges don't care what excuses you have. My time off has to be planned months in advance."

Danny sighed. "I know. And I'm not asking you to stop what you're doing. In fact, I need you where you are. You're safe in courthouses. You still have a gun at home?"

"Yes."

"Good. Keep it on your nightstand while you sleep. Check your surroundings anytime you leave the house. I can't imagine they would kidnap you a second time, especially since they have my mom already. What more leverage could they possibly need?"

"I'm glad we're on the same page." Nadia sighed. Was that relief or frustration? Danny had trouble reading Nadia's moods lately. "Danny, I know I said I didn't want to get dragged into your drama, but we have to get your mom back. This doesn't sit right with me, and I really wish you'd let me contact the police. Or the FBI. I have contacts, you know."

"It's me they want. And it's me they'll get. No outsiders. What else did their messages say?"

"The messages eventually stopped," she said. "They called me this morning."

"Why on earth would they do that?"

"They were upset I wasn't responding to the texts. Had to guarantee I was getting the message."

"Did they make any threats against you?"

"None. Only against you. They're just using me to pressure you into playing their games. You can expect a call from them at some point today. They made it plenty clear your mom's life is in danger if you don't comply with their demands."

"Did they mention the list of names they sent me?"

"No. What names?"

"Zak is looking into it for me. But his was on the list."

Nadia groaned. "I don't like this, Danny. Something about this time feels more serious. I pressed them for answers about your mom and where she is, but they wouldn't tell me a damned thing. I threatened to call the FBI, and they laughed."

"Was it a man on the phone call?"

"I think so. It's possible a woman used a voice changer, but I don't think that's what happened. Seemed like a man intentionally speaking in a deeper voice."

Danny swore. "If they call me today, I'm going to make a deal. I'll do whatever they want if they agree to release my mom. No reason for her to spend another second wherever they're holding her."

"Then what, Danny?" Her voice was filled with sympathy, concern. Danny's heart melted from it. "You going to put her back in that home in Aspen? Take care of her yourself?"

Nadia was right. She usually was. Danny had become too focused on getting his desired outcome that he hadn't thought of what life might look like after. If he got his mother back this afternoon, what *would* he do?

He couldn't bring her to live in a hotel room, nor would he take her to her house in Denver. These evil men were still out there, and Danny couldn't trust anything until all guilty parties were behind bars.

Tatiana was also becoming more immobile. Long road trips were out of the question. Hell, even a flight across the country could prove too exhausting for her.

They were shackled by her failing health. Danny supposed he could find a rental property somewhere else in the state. But how long would it be until they found them again? Plus, whatever deal he made with these goons would require some of his time. He couldn't leave his mother alone for more than an hour. That had been the point of her living in a retirement home, after all.

"Danny?" Nadia's voice brought him back to the disturbing reality facing him.

"Sorry. I don't know what I'll do," he said, "but I need her back by my side. It's not like these people are taking care of her properly. She needs professional care, and I'll do whatever I can to make that happen."

Nadia was silent for a moment. Danny almost thought she'd left the call until she said, "There is another option. But I'm not sure how you'll feel about it."

"Everything's on the table right now. Try me."

"Some assisted living facilities have suites with multiple bedrooms meant for the children to live with their parents. That way you could come and go as you please—and she'll be cared for—and you'll be present with her whenever you're home."

Danny considered this. Living in an assisted living facility? The initial thought was almost laughable. But the more he weighed it, the more intriguing it became. Those facilities had security protocols.

It wouldn't be as possible for something similar to happen again, not if Danny was a resident of the same facility. No fake phone call could send his mother away. They'd have to hear it from him, a fellow resident, in person.

But living in a facility where everyone was deteriorating? With the trouble that followed Danny every step he took? He wouldn't put only his mother at risk, but other innocent people as well. People trying to live out their last days on this planet with as much peace as they could find.

"That's an interesting thought," Danny said. "I'll need to think that over. Of course, a lot of that depends on what happens. But it's good knowing that's an option. Thank you."

If he had done such a thing from the outset, would he have gotten tangled in the mess with Villa after the drug lord had escaped from prison in the first place? Would they have found him, or gotten close enough to threaten his way of life?

Danny's stomach twisted at the thought. Of course they would have. That's how the cartel functioned. If they wanted someone, they didn't stop until they got them.

"You're welcome," Nadia said. "I need to get back to work, but I'll be in touch, okay? And so should you. They're going to call you today. Please don't rush into any decisions you'll regret later. There are other ways to find your mom, aside from selling your soul to the devil."

"Thanks again. I don't want you to worry about any of this unless you hear from me. I'll take care of this myself."

And now, Danny faced an entirely different beast. More powerful than the cartel. More vicious than any mobster.

The United States government.

CHAPTER SIX

NIKO FELLNER LIT a cigarette and drew in a hearty puff of smoke.

It had been a busy year so far, and they weren't even halfway through it. The boss kept him around, even after the fiasco in New Mexico that had seen Victor Villa return to prison. The entire purpose of Niko's job was to keep Villa *out* of prison. He never understood why the boss insisted on keeping a bloodthirsty criminal on the streets, but Niko wasn't paid to ask questions.

Besides, the boss saw plenty of value in what Niko brought to the table. Aside from being one of the most feared assassins in Germany, Niko understood logistics at a detailed level that would make the most analytical person drool.

Before his days as an assassin, Niko worked for the Frankfurt mafia, overseeing the import of cocaine and heroin. Niko created the distribution system that had made the mafia the most powerful in Germany, and eventually Austria. Those twelve years had taught Niko everything he knew.

When the police started arresting other members of the mafia, Niko fled Germany and never looked back, settling in Virginia where he'd found government contract work in shipping logistics.

He worked his way up the ranks and shook hands with the right people. It didn't take long—about two years—before Niko met a man who'd wished to remain anonymous. But the man had insisted he had power and influence in Washington. Could change Niko's life forever.

Niko had his doubts, but the envelopes full of cash left on his doorstep after each job allowed him to quit his job and work full time for "the boss."

He hadn't seen the boss in person since their first encounter, and they primarily communicated via an app called Vanish. It worked as an instant messaging service that deleted any message after it was read.

Niko had assumed this work would eventually cross a legal line. And it did. Kidnappings. Robberies. Spying. And the occasional murder. All done stealthily. All accomplished with the confidence of a man assured nothing would ever be tied to him.

The boss promised Niko's name would be scrubbed from every database within the US government, erasing his presence in the country. The boss had also stayed true to his word about keeping plenty of space between himself, Niko, and any of the targets. Niko could just as easily do the work he was asked to oversee, but that meant his direct involvement. The boss couldn't risk Niko getting caught and ending up in the judicial system. Or worse, deported back to Germany.

Niko knew little about the targets of his assigned missions. He'd receive a message, or several, with instructions about a target's last known whereabouts, and what was expected of Niko. Most jobs were straightforward. Locating a target and spying on them for a week to understand their routines would get Niko anywhere between ten thousand and thirty thousand dollars, depending on the duration of the job.

Killing a target in the shadows of the night would net him at least a hundred and fifty thousand. His envelope arrived just yesterday for the kidnapping of an elderly woman from her assisted living community. Ninety-five thousand dollars for simply orchestrating the kidnapping. Niko never stepped foot in Colorado but had the perfect crew to recruit for the job. He'd made the calls to kick things into motion, studied the area with satellite mapping, and planned every detail from the time of the crew's arrival to their eventual departure and escape across the country.

Niko considered his work to be mostly simple. Arrange matters, send out instructions, sit back, and watch it all come together. His current assignment, however, had several moving pieces. The boss needed certain people eliminated but having them all merely executed would draw suspicions. His grand idea was to have them kill each other. Make it appear like there was turmoil and mistrust among the group.

Blackmail one into killing another and keep going until they're all gone. Self-elimination.

That was one of the first messages Niko had received about a Danny Cortez from Colorado. Danny might have ended up in the good graces of the boss had he just killed Victor Villa. But the ex-DEA agent had left him behind for the authorities to toss back behind bars.

"And now we're here," Niko whispered to himself, studying a picture of Danny Cortez on his computer screen.

They planned to use the elderly woman, Danny's mother, to drive him into killing as many people on the list as they could get away with. Once Danny reached his peak, Niko would blackmail someone else into killing Danny. Round and round they'd go, and the cash envelopes would keep arriving.

So many in Niko's line of work rushed into decisions. The looming threat of the law made people act irrationally. Niko recognized complex plans required precise timing. If the smallest piece was out of place, Niko had no problem calling off the entire job until everything was perfect.

He could have called Danny last night, or even earlier this morning. But to blackmail someone into killing for you, well, that required desperation. The longer Danny went without knowing his mother was okay would only increase that desperation.

Judging enough time had passed, Niko picked up his cell phone—gifted by the boss, of course—and dialed Danny's burner phone number that had taken them six weeks to track down.

"Who is this?" Danny answered.

Niko smiled. He was a soft-spoken man, but deepened his voice when speaking to targets. "Good afternoon, Mr. Cortez. You don't need to know my name. Only what I have to offer."

"I don't care about your offer. Where is my mother?"

"Your mother is in good hands, Mr. Cortez. You don't need to worry about her. She is alive and well. She is with two former nurses who specialize in dementia care. They have no reason to harm your mother and will give her just as much care and attention—if not more—than what she was receiving at Morning Star."

"Where is she?!" Danny demanded. His voice filled with rage, and Niko grinned once more. Rage was desperation's sexy cousin.

"Her location doesn't matter," Niko said. "She is safe and will be released as soon as you complete some work for me."

Niko heard the faint sound of Danny tapping the screen on his phone.

"Texting someone?" Niko asked.

"None of your damn business what I'm doing. What do you need me to do?"

So quick to obey. Niko hadn't even threatened anything yet. "You received a text message with a list of names. I need those people removed, and you're just the guy for the job."

"I'm no assassin."

"Not yet. But you're a sharpshooter who understands stealth. That's really all you need. I'll provide you with the rest of the details. Even the best time to approach your targets to ensure you won't be caught. I'm even willing to compensate you for your travel, as you'll be visiting plenty of different cities across the country."

"And who are these people on the list? Criminals? Surely you can't force me to kill innocent people."

"No one is forcing you to do anything, Mr. Cortez. You still have free rein to do as you please. But we negotiate in good faith. Should you not complete the request, I can't promise your mother will continue to receive the stellar care she currently has."

The phone crunched as Danny squeezed it. "Say I agree to this. Are you really expecting me to kill all those names on the list? I just don't see how it's fair to hold my mother's life hostage so I can kill five people. Five for one isn't exactly a fair trade."

"Life's not fair, Mr. Cortez. All you can do is accept the offer in front of you. Or not. Now, do we have a deal?"

The line remained silent for nearly a minute, but Niko knew the call was still connected. Again, patience. Others would force their targets to give an answer. But not Niko. He'd sit on the line for three hours if that's what it took. The more time that passed, the more desperate Mr. Cortez would become.

Danny finally cleared his throat. "I'll do this first one. But after that, I want to speak to my mom. If I don't get to, you can forget about me killing anyone else."

A negotiator. Those were rare in Niko's line of work. Most people just agreed to the terms to get what they wanted.

"I can arrange that for you, Mr. Cortez."

"If you don't, I'll hunt you down and make you pay."

Niko chuckled. "I'm sure you will, Mr. Cortez. Your first target is Marcus Vance. He lives in Texas. Would you prefer to fly or drive?"

CHAPTER SEVEN

DANNY REFUSED the man's dirty money and drove himself to Denton, Texas, overnight.

He'd visited Texas plenty of times throughout his life. Had even lived there for a six-month assignment in Austin.

Danny had plenty of conversations with himself during the twelve-hour drive, mainly about how he preferred to approach this situation. He had no intention of killing a man in cold blood to save his mother, but he couldn't tell that to the man who'd called him.

He'd have to do what came naturally and wing it when he arrived. He'd keep a safe distance away from his target upon arrival. Scout him for a few days and devise a plan to satisfy the deep-voiced man on the phone. Danny told himself—yet didn't fully believe—that if Marcus Vance displayed any sort of negative actions, like abusing a wife or child, Danny would proceed with the assassination.

His conscience would battle that decision if the time came.

Danny pulled into Denton at 5:30 in the morning and parked outside a Holiday Inn.

After killing his engine, he dialed Zak's burner phone and rolled down the window to let in the fresh air.

"Good morning, Danny," Zak answered. "A bit early for you, isn't it?"

"I just arrived in Denton, Texas, after driving all night. Forgive me if I'm a little out of it."

"What the hell are you doing in Texas?"

"Nothing you need to worry about. I need your help. Do you still have access to phone records?"

"Sure do. Steele hasn't taken that away yet. Still wants me to do my job, I suppose."

"I received a disturbing call yesterday. I dialed star-five-seven toward the end, so you shouldn't need a warrant to pull the data from Verizon."

"And the call was placed to this same number? Do you have the time?"

"Yes. Call came in at 3:07 p.m. Mountain time."

"Got it. I'll see what I can find. These requests can take several days, especially because I can't position it as an urgent matter—that would need approval from Steele. But I'll do what I can."

"Thanks, Zak. I don't mind waiting. Just want to know where the call came from. Might help me narrow down some things."

"You sure everything's okay?" Zak asked after a beat. "Did the call have anything to do with your mom?"

"It had everything to do with her."

"Christ, Danny. Don't do something you'll regret. There are other ways to get your mom back."

Why did everyone keep saying that? Like he could just call the police, open an investigation, and they would know where to go. Danny believed someone in the government was operating this scheme. If the government wanted someone to go missing, then good luck finding them. Danny spent enough years in the DEA to know how it all worked. Paperwork. Warrants. Dealing with judges. So many steps to simply gain permission to investigate a certain location or person.

His mother didn't have the luxury of time. At her last doctor's visit, they'd predicted Tatiana Cortez had less than a year left.

And Danny had seen it. She'd become so frail. Helpless. Her daily confusion forced him to bury his face in his pillow and let out the tears.

His mother, as he knew and remembered, was already gone. Wherever she was, Danny doubted she even remembered leaving Morning Star.

That's what pissed him off so much. Criminals picking on helpless individuals for their selfish gains. He didn't care what the schmuck on the phone said about them taking care of his mom. They had no right to interfere with her life.

Danny brushed these thoughts aside and unfolded the piece of paper where he had written Marcus Vance's home address. He still half expected the whole thing to be a hoax. Maybe an ambush to capture Danny.

But the list of names was too intentional. And why not force Danny into killing people? He already had a negative reputation within the U.S. government. It wouldn't be a stretch for them to slander his name in a courtroom while he stood trial for murder.

I'm not killing anyone. Not today.

Danny plugged the address into his phone's GPS and made the three-minute drive to the next neighborhood over. It was almost six o'clock. The man on the phone had already provided a schedule of events for Marcus Vance, and noted he typically woke up at 6:15 to brew a cup of coffee for him and his wife and help see his teens out the door to school.

Danny entered the neighborhood of Northridge, finding ranch-style homes all made of brick. Lots of wide, green lawns. American flags hung from nearly every house.

Despite the early hour, a few landscaping crews were already at work on the lawns, likely eager to beat the afternoon heat. Danny turned onto Magnolia Street and rolled to a stop across the road from the Vance residence.

Vance's house resembled every other on the block. A pristine lawn with a garden along the sidewalk. The man had said Vance was retired, so there would be plenty of opportunities to get him alone and "carry out the work."

The morning sun cast its glow over the neighborhood. At 6:15 sharp, a light on the left side of the house turned on.

His bedroom.

The light remained on for only two minutes before it turned back off. Danny waited another twenty minutes before the kitchen light illuminated. With no curtains or blinds, Danny had his first glimpse of Marcus Vance. And he was just as the man on the phone had described. Tall. Athletic. Thick-framed glasses and short gray hair slicked to the side.

Vance fidgeted with the coffee machine before pouring himself a bowl of cereal. Shortly after, he sat at the kitchen table with his breakfast and cell phone. Two lights on the right-hand side of the house flicked on. Moments later, two teenagers wandered into the kitchen. The girl gave her father a hug, and the boy patted him on the back. They conversed for a couple of minutes before the teens disappeared back to their rooms.

Danny sighed through his nose. So far everything the man had told him was true. It was both reassuring and frightening. If they already had such accurate details on Marcus Vance and his routine, why did they need Danny to carry out their dirty work? Surely they could find people more qualified than him to carry out an assassination.

The next hour made Danny nauseous. Vance's kids joined him at the breakfast table, dressed and ready for the day. They poured cereal and chatted with their father before packing their lunches and heading out the door.

If Danny returned for a second day, he'd follow the kids. The man had said they left for school, but it was the middle of June. Maybe it was a summer camp or something else. But the two kids left together.

Shortly after their departure, Vance's wife joined him in the kitchen, still wearing her nightgown. They shared a kiss, and he poured a cup of coffee for her. They sat together and talked for ten minutes while she sipped from her steaming mug. After that, she left the kitchen, and Vance cooked eggs, bacon, and toast. He plated the food and served it to his wife when she returned, now dressed.

It wasn't until she finished eating that Vance finally left the kitchen. Ten minutes later, their garage door opened, and he appeared outside with gardening gloves, a rake, and a small bag of soil. For the next hour, Vance tended to his garden. He pulled weeds. Sprayed chemicals. Planted new seeds. Hand-watered the flowers that already thrived.

All the while bobbing his head along to whatever music played in his headphones. Danny drew in a deep breath and blew it out of his mouth. After heading back inside, Vance returned to the kitchen, where his wife had finished squeezing lemons into a jug of water. They laughed and danced in the kitchen, ending with a long hug and brief make-out session.

"What in the world?" Danny asked himself. "*This* is the guy they want me to kill?"

It may have only been a couple of hours of observation, but Danny discovered no reason warranting the death of Marcus Vance. A family man living in the suburbs of Dallas. Minding his business. Caring for those he loved. Danny had seen plenty of criminals in his life, and not one of them had a morning routine like Marcus Vance's.

Having seen enough, Danny turned on his truck and left the neighborhood for his hotel. One thought weighed on his mind.

No way in hell I'm killing that man.

CHAPTER EIGHT

AFTER CHECKING into his hotel later that morning, fatigue settled in. Danny took a ninety-minute nap to recharge. Starving, as his last meal had been a burger from a McDonald's in Kansas, he'd caught the end of the continental breakfast and filled up on fruit and pastries.

By the time he woke up, the thought of Marcus Vance was a distant dream. Nothing made sense, and he refused to carry out the mystery man's twisted orders. But riding his high horse wouldn't get his mother released.

Danny had no idea if it would work, but he opened his phone's call records and called back the restricted number. It rang several times before the man eventually answered. Danny didn't buy his deep voice this time.

"Hello?" the man said. "Who is this?"

"Not used to getting calls back, are you?" Danny replied. "You probably think you can push people around to do what you say. But I'm not that way, little man. So I suggest you listen."

"Mr. Cortez?"

"Don't play games with me. You expect me to believe you would answer the phone if you didn't know who was on the other end? Shut up and listen."

"Mister—"

"I'm in Texas right now. Watched Marcus Vance earlier this morning. I literally watched him scoop a spider out of his garden and place it on his lawn. You must be out of your mind if you think I'm going to kill him. Whatever reason you have for sending this man to his death is nonsense. Clearly, this is a personal vendetta. If you want him dead, kill him yourself. Are we clear?"

"Can I speak now, Mr. Cortez?"

Danny could sense the smirk on the man's face and longed for the day when he would wipe it off. "Speak, asshole."

"Mr. Cortez. I appreciate your concern for Mr. Vance. And you're absolutely correct. He's a good man. Shame he needs to be eliminated, but we all have our orders. I would kill him myself, but my boss doesn't want me getting my hands dirty. I'm more of a behind-the-scenes guy. My killing days are over. But don't think I couldn't handle the job if I needed to."

"Well, you do. Because it's not going to be me."

The man laughed. "You misunderstood, Mr. Cortez. I'm not killing Marcus Vance. That's your job."

"No, *sir. You* misunderstood. I'm not killing that man. Do what you must with my mother. That will be on your conscience. Not mine."

Now the man chuckled, and Danny craved nothing more than to reach through the phone and clench his throat until the last drop of air escaped his lungs. "It is quite lethal to call a bluff when it is, in fact, not a bluff."

"I'm not calling a bluff," Danny said. "I know what little men like you will do. If I need to accept my losses and move on, I will. I'm only a few hours from the border. I can vanish into Mexico, and you'll never find me again."

The man laughed again. "That's a cute image, Mr. Cortez. But I suggest you look at the bigger picture before rushing into any decisions. See, this is about more than just your mother. We only took her to provide that initial shock to your system. We have plenty of other options to deploy, should you not comply with our demands."

"Who are you working for?" Danny demanded, remaining calm despite the panic unleashing in his thoughts.

They're going to take Nadia next if I don't make a move.

"That's none of your business," the man said. "Nor mine, apparently."

"Are you saying you don't know who you're working for?"

"Precisely. I receive jobs which I then … delegate. And once a job is done, money arrives on my doorstep."

"So, if you went missing, say you fled to Mexico with me. Who would know? How would they find you?"

The man cackled. "As tempting as that romantic getaway sounds, I'm afraid you're wasting your breath. I have no reason to leave. I've built a life I love doing this work. No complaints, aside from occasional headaches. You know a thing or two about that."

"Humor me. If I disappear today, what will happen next?"

"In regard to Mr. Vance, or to those you love? I'll address both. I'd hire someone else to eliminate Mr. Vance. That's not a problem. You're mistaken if you think you're the only hired gun I've reached out to. But see, that's the boring part of the job. Mr. Vance will go missing in the middle of the night. Police will investigate, but they'll find nothing. And we all move on with our lives after a couple of weeks. That's the offer currently on your table."

Danny hadn't unpacked much upon his arrival but started repacking his bag to leave the hotel. After this phone call, he wasn't entirely sure what he'd do. But he wouldn't waste the day sitting around the Holiday Inn.

The man continued. "The fun part would be dealing with you for your refusal to obey orders. First off, we'd kill your mother. Now, I can't say how gruesome it would be. The crew she's with has a soft spot for dementia patients, so they might take the easy way and slip her a lethal injection. No pain. No fuss. Unless they're feeling frisky at the time. Hard to say. But think of all the creative activities you could perform on someone bound to a wheelchair. Maybe a late-night stroll into the ocean?"

Ocean. They're on a coastline.

"Once your mother is out of the picture, we'd shift our focus to that pretty girl you're always talking to in Chicago. Nadia, right?" Danny's skin prickled at the mention of her. These guys really covered all their bases. "We know it would be trickier, considering her high profile in that city, but we can make it work. Pay off some judges, have them look the other way. Once we have Nadia, the games will really begin. Probably cut off a finger and mail it to you. Even in Mexico. We'll find you. Doesn't matter where in the world you try to hide. We have eyes everywhere."

Danny seethed through the line. "Nadia has nothing to do with this."

"And neither does your mother," the man said. "But *you* do. All you have to do is carry out the plans I've given you. Anyway, we'd keep Nadia for a while. Maybe a month or two. See if that brings you back into the picture. Once her phase is done, we'll move on to your childhood home. Trash it. Send you pictures. Damage your family mementos. Would be a shame if all your father's war medals went missing. I'm sure a local pawn shop would have a field day with those. After all that, if you still refused to comply, we'd burn the house down."

Danny clenched his jaw so tight his teeth hurt.

"Then, and only then. Once your house and childhood memories are nothing more than a pile of rubble and ash, we will come for you. Wherever you're hiding. Our assassins will find you. And they'll have instructions to make your death painful and excruciating. And for a trained assassin, I'm not entirely sure what that means to them. Torture is subjective, wouldn't you say? So go ahead, Mr. Cortez. Cross that border into Mexico. Sip your margaritas on the beach. You'll get a post-card from me soon enough."

Danny remained silent. He needed to get his rage under control before blurting out anything he might regret. This man, and whoever he worked for, understood how to play hardball. Danny couldn't deny that the threats had gotten to him.

Still, they couldn't break through his morality. He wouldn't kill Marcus Vance, no matter what they threw his way.

The man kept quiet, but Danny heard his distant breathing over the line. Danny had a plan but needed to iron out some details in his mind first.

"Tell me your name," Danny said, buying himself more time. "It's the least you can do."

"I really shouldn't do that, Mr. Cortez. I'm sure you can understand."

"Tell me your name. Give me a fake name. Just give me something I can call you. I'm sure *you* can understand."

Without having met this man in person, Danny hated him more than anyone he could recall in recent memory. Not even Victor Villa played mind games this twisted.

"Very well," the man finally said. "You can call me Niko."

"Fine then, Niko. Message received. I'll do your killings for you, but I want to do them my way. There's just something about you I don't trust. Think I can get away with it better than by doing it your way."

"My instructions are merely suggestions. You are more than welcome to do as you please. We only care about the results."

"And results are what you'll get," Danny said. "Give me a day to think this over. I'll be in touch."

CHAPTER NINE

DANNY LEFT the hotel two minutes after hanging up with Niko.

Niko had said plenty during their call, but nothing more important than his subtle revelation he was near an ocean. It made sense. If he was working for the government, most of their offices were out in the D.C. area. Virginia. Maryland. While few people thought of those locations as prime beach destinations, the Atlantic Ocean lay right there.

Danny wished he could have driven east without a worry, but Niko had gotten to him. The threats against his mother and Nadia were enough to make him look over his shoulder whenever stepping foot in public.

What pressed on Danny's mind were the words from Nadia and Zak.

There are other ways to get your mom back.

And there were.

Danny had briefly considered calling the police, but he had developed enough contacts within the federal government that he didn't need to rely on local police departments to get answers. Zak was working on tracing the call with Niko, and he wouldn't dare ask him to do more. Not with eyes on him.

But Danny wondered, as thorough as Niko and his crew appeared, did they really have no idea Danny and Zak were still friends? Or did they not care? Maybe part of their twisted game was to make Danny kill his friend. They had no issue stretching the limits of right and wrong.

Aside from Zak, Danny had more contacts within the DEA. And a few in the FBI.

Danny had an idea that just might work to get Niko off his tail and allow him to travel east in search of his mother.

He'd spent plenty of time at the FBI offices in Dallas while working a joint case with them six years ago. A drug ring that also ran a human trafficking business.

He didn't know if any of the agents he had worked with were still in Dallas. But he'd march through the doors and drop names until someone invited him up to their desk.

Once inside, Danny would call Niko back, all while the FBI helped trace the call live. It would be up to them what they did after that. Hopefully, they could make a quick call out east and have their agents arrest Niko and demand answers.

Danny's stomach twisted with anticipation. His next trip could be to merely pick up his mother and bring her home without killing Marcus Vance or anyone else on that list. Even if the FBI couldn't help immediately, Danny figured he'd bought himself at least a day—he never said *when* he would call Niko back.

His confidence soaring, Danny arrived at the FBI offices and parked a block away. Their main lot was fenced off and guarded by an elderly man in a booth. Danny wouldn't have had an issue getting past him, maybe tell a story about forgetting his badge. But he believed fate came with limits. And his primary concern was getting into the actual offices.

His heart raced as he turned off the engine and drew in a deep breath. "Sam Murillo. Jessica Adams. Robert Yamamoto."

Danny recited the three names of the FBI agents he had worked with all those years ago. It was a long shot all three of them still worked in the same office, but if just one did, he could talk his way into meeting with them and pleading his case.

His cell phone rang just as he was about to step out of the truck. Zak.

"Hello?" Danny answered, his anxiety climbing. "Hello? Zak?"

The call dropped, and Danny gazed at his phone. *Do I call him back? Did he have to hang up right away to not get caught?*

Too much uncertainty floated around every action and decision. As much as he wished to call Zak back, Danny resisted out of fear. Zak worked in the same building as Charles Steele. If the radical DEA Administrator so much as stepped out of his office and peered in Zak's direction, Danny couldn't blame his friend for ending the call before speaking.

Everyone involved had to tiptoe around getting caught.

If Zak fell out of line, who knew what might happen? Especially with his name already on the list. If Steele caught him leaking inside information to Danny, he'd eliminate Zak himself and scramble to devise a new plan.

"Expose them," Danny said to his empty truck. "Expose them all and take them down. They can't get away with this forever."

Danny waited another five minutes in the truck to see if Zak would call back. When he didn't, Danny slipped the phone back into his pocket and stepped out on the sidewalk.

Heat radiated from the asphalt in a suffocating wave. He was a long way from Aspen, where they had no understanding of how cruel summer could be.

Danny had parked around the corner, out of sight from the FBI offices, and stood in front of what appeared to be an old electronics store. Boards covered the windows, graffiti markings added to the decor. Tattered remains of a "Going out of business" sign clung to the glass door. Through the door he saw empty shelves, a knocked-over ladder, and litter scattered about the floor.

Further down, Danny spotted a busy sandwich shop. But on his corner of the block, Danny strolled through a ghost town.

After this visit with the FBI, everything will change for the better.

Danny marched forward, convinced of this simple truth. Before reaching the corner of the block to turn right, two black vans screeched down the street and slammed on their brakes directly in front of Danny.

His phone buzzed again in his pocket, but Danny never felt it. Not with his adrenaline kicking into high gear. He had a split second to decide his next move. He could turn and run. Be caught by one of the two vans. His truck was within reach, but could he get behind the wheel before the vans boxed him in?

Danny had no time to decide, and the van's sliding doors opened, revealing several people in black uniforms. They jumped out, three with assault rifles fixed on Danny.

"Daniel Cortez?" one asked.

Danny stepped back and reached into his pocket. He wanted to call Zak. Call Niko. Call anyone who could get him out of whatever these people had planned.

"Drop the phone!" the man shouted.

Danny lit up his screen and found a text message.

ZAK

The number belongs to the CIA.

His gut sank. The man who had called out his name stepped forward with his rifle and smacked the phone out of Danny's hand with the gun's muzzle.

"What the hell?!" Danny shouted.

A man in a suit climbed out from the van, sunglasses concealing his gaze as he glanced around at the scene.

"Weapons down," he said in an irritated voice. He approached Danny, reaching into his suit jacket to grab a badge, which he promptly flashed at Danny. "Mr. Cortez, I'm Special Agent Larry Richards with the CIA. We need you to come with us so we can ask you some questions."

Danny froze. "Am I in some sort of trouble?"

His heart hammered against his ribcage. The guns may have been lowered, but Danny sensed a dark turn of events on the immediate horizon.

"You're Danny Cortez, right? Former DEA agent who helped capture Victor Villa in New Mexico earlier this year?"

"Yes—"

"Perfect. We need a word with you. In private."

"Okay. Can I follow you to an office?"

"No, sir," Richards said. "We are running a stealth operation. You'll need to come with us."

Danny laughed. "You must be out of your mind. If you had any clue what I've been dealing with these past two days—"

"We do," Richards said. "Your mother's been kidnapped, and you're out here in Texas to kill a man named Marcus Vance. Right?"

"How…yes, that's correct."

"Get in the van, Mr. Cortez."

CHAPTER TEN

DANNY REGRETTED GETTING into the van the instant he sat down.

The CIA agents—if that's what they really were—all sat across from him with their faces covered by tactical balaclavas. No one spoke a word, except for Special Agent Richards assuring Danny he was safe and everything was fine.

Danny knew better. Safety didn't need to be explained unless you were trying to lull someone into a false sense of security. These people had jumped out of a van with their guns drawn. That wasn't the sign of someone wanting a quick chat. Those rifles were cocked and ready to fire if Danny had made any sudden movements.

Richards had scooped up Danny's cell phone and promised to give it back when they were finished.

After the drive had lasted ten minutes, Danny asked, "Where are we going?"

Dallas is a big city. It'd take another thirty minutes for them to be outside of the limits.

"Private facility," Richards replied. "We have a long drive ahead. Maybe an hour."

We're heading into the middle of nowhere.

And why wouldn't they? Take Danny into the heat of the Texas desert, ask him some questions, and shoot him in the head when they were finished.

There were too many pieces of the puzzle missing, however, and Danny didn't know how much he could trust these people who picked him up.

"How did you know about my mom?" he asked. "And how did you find me?"

Richards cleared his throat. "All will be explained when we arrive. Don't worry about the details."

If Richards was on Danny's side, he would have already shared this information. They were in private, and he doubted the foot soldiers Richards brought along didn't already know what was going on.

"Do you work for him?" Danny asked. "Or with him?"

Richards appeared amused by the question, his mouth curling into a smirk. "With whom?"

Danny shrugged. "Niko? If that's his real name."

"Niko." Richards leaned his head back and stared at the van's ceiling. "I don't know any Niko. We work for the CIA."

"So you've said. I wasn't aware the CIA picked up innocent civilians off the street."

Richards' grin widened. "Don't act like you're some regular Joe out on his coffee break. You have a past. Knowledge. What were you doing anyway? Planning on visiting the FBI, I presume? And what were you going to tell them?"

"Is that why you came for me in such a panic?" Danny asked. "Worried I was going to blow your scheme?"

Richards laughed. "As a matter of fact, yes. Now, it's not what you think, but we can't afford any…complications. If the FBI looked into your claims, they'd find things that would prompt them to ask questions of the wrong people."

"What people?"

"I've said too much already. You'll get more answers when we arrive. In fact, there is a special someone waiting for you there, and I'm sure he'll be more than pleased to address any of your concerns."

Danny asked through gritted teeth, "Do you know where my mother is?"

"Afraid not. I only know she is being held hostage until you take care of your business. I'll tell you this much, Mr. Cortez. If you do as they ask, they really do release their hostages. You can have your mother back in no time."

Danny let silence replace the conversation. Richards was a criminal, just like Niko and whoever the hell they were both working for. Probably the same person. He didn't trust the man sitting across from him, and recognized he hid plenty more information.

Assuming I get out of here alive, I need to head east and find my mom. No phone. No GPS. That's obviously how they knew where I was today.

The drive suddenly became bumpy, causing everyone to sway in their seats. A dirt road. Danny had driven on plenty.

They continued for the next thirty minutes, while Danny calculated the best route for him from Dallas to D.C. If he could meet with Zak in person, his friend might point him in the right direction. He'd already discovered Niko's phone number linked to the CIA offices.

Another reason Danny didn't believe a word coming from Richards' lips.

"Almost there," Richards finally said, reaching into his suit jacket to pull out a container of breath mints, popping two in his mouth.

"Hot date tonight?" Danny asked.

Richards grinned. "You haven't formally asked me yet."

"Sorry, sweetie, you're not my type."

Richards chuckled and glanced around at his goons. They all remained still and showed no signs of acknowledging the conversation between their leader and prisoner.

Am I a prisoner? They haven't cuffed me.

Danny took this for mutual trust. If he didn't harm them, they wouldn't harm him. Maybe they really did plan to let him go after whatever questioning they had was over. Or maybe it was another layer of false security. They wanted him to trust them right up to the moment he turned around to leave their facility when they'd put a bullet in the back of his skull.

The bumping stopped as the van returned to a flat surface. They rolled to a stop, muffled voices coming from the front of the van while they sat there for two stifling minutes. As they drove forward again,

Danny's nerves subsided. These people were going to help him or kill him. Either option led to definitive closure.

"We're here," Richards said when the van came to a stop again. He leaned forward, his minty breath wafting into Danny's nose. "Now listen up. We've brought you here in confidence. We trust you'll do the right thing. Listen to what everyone has to say. You'll be meeting with important people, all of whom want to help you get your mother back. You're familiar with working in the federal government, so you should know everyone is just taking orders from someone else. That's no different for me or with the man you'll soon be speaking with. Keep that in mind."

Danny shook his head. "We're all puppets obeying the man pulling the strings."

"Precisely."

Danny rubbed his temples. People like Richards frustrated him. You couldn't luck your way into the CIA. You had to have the goods. Intelligence. Bravery. And a high degree of stealth. Any trait these three-letter agencies liked to put in their mottos.

Richards had these traits but had clearly fallen into a trap. Some people grew complacent after too many years on the job and preferred to coast along by doing whatever was asked of them. Others became brainwashed, convinced obeying orders would help them move up the ranks.

Danny had several reasons for leaving the DEA, and this was one of them. Those who remained strong-minded and independent were eventually shown the door or moved to entirely different departments. They would bounce around the federal workforce for a few years before realizing they could never actually move upward. It was all a trap, and one Danny had no intention of falling into.

Then there were people like Zak. The unicorns. Zak remained independent and strong-willed but understood the game and adapted. He gave the appearance of obeying orders, all while making things happen on his own. Agents like him received promotions. Danny never went to any of the unofficial gatherings, but Zak did. He greased palms, networked with others, and played the game to perfection.

"If all goes well in here," Richards said, "you'll get to leave. And once you do, you cannot discuss anything you see here today or the consequences will be unbearable."

"Sounds like a good time."

The door slid open and the other agents filed out, leaving Danny alone with Richards. "I'm serious, Mr. Cortez. Nothing here is a joke. Now, follow me."

Danny followed Richards out of the van and stepped onto a concrete floor. He peered around to see they were inside a massive warehouse. In the distance, dozens of people worked on assembly lines. Danny couldn't tell what they were doing.

Closer to Danny's left was a row of offices and conference rooms.

Richards started toward these and motioned for Danny to follow. The offices had frosted windows, revealing distorted shapes moving around inside. The conference rooms had regular glass, and Danny was relieved Richards took him into one of those.

A table with twelve plush pleather chairs occupied the middle of the room, a 100-inch television hanging on the wall.

"Please have a seat, Mr. Cortez." Richards gestured at the empty chairs. "Your interview will begin in just a moment. There's a fridge in the back of the room with a selection of cold drinks. Help yourself. We'll talk soon."

Richards bowed out of the room and closed the door behind him without another word.

Danny visited the fridge to grab two bottles of water. He unscrewed the lid and gulped until he felt like himself again.

When the door flew open, Danny nearly dropped his water bottle.

"Danny Cortez," the man said. "Long time, no see. Have a seat. We have a lot to discuss."

Danny immediately doubted his odds of leaving this warehouse alive as he sat down, unable to peel his gaze off the man at the other end of the table.

The man who dropped into a chair and plonked his feet on the table was none other than DEA Administrator, Charles Steele.

CHAPTER ELEVEN

THE LAST TIME Danny saw Chuck Steele, they were colleagues at the DEA.

While Danny had worked as an intelligence analyst, Steele had the title of Chief of Operations—third in command within the administration.

Their paths rarely crossed before Danny's old partner, Dexter Jordan, was kidnapped by Victor Villa's cartel. After that incident, Danny had met with Steele regularly to discuss the events of that day.

Now he sat across the table from Danny, the office's bright lights gleaming off his bald head, a cocky smirk plastered on his face.

What does he know? Is Zak okay? If they caught him talking to me, Steele could have vanished him without a second thought.

Danny had long held suspicions the DEA was involved with Victor Villa. In what capacity, he couldn't say. But it went beyond the fugitive/captor relationship it should have been.

"Long time, Danny." Steele leaned further back in his seat, his feet still perched on the table. He crossed his hands behind his head. "Can't lie, I'm surprised you're still out here trucking along. Thought you would've run as far from this life as you could."

"Chuck." Danny refused to show him the respect of calling him Mr. Steele.

The man across the table had long left a sour taste in Danny's mouth. After months of an internal investigation, Steele had proposed —along with a handful of other theories—Dexter's kidnapping was Danny's fault. An independent panel of judges had found no merit in the accusation and dropped the charges, but Steele had burned the bridge. Danny never trusted him again.

"Why were you poking around the FBI office today?" Steele asked.

"Why were you visiting Dallas at the same time as me?" Danny countered. "Suspicious timing, considering."

"You're not the one asking questions today. Answer mine, and maybe I'll answer some of yours. If you refuse, well, you may as well get comfortable here."

Rage flushed Danny's face, but he couldn't act on it. Not yet. "I was going to the FBI to tell them I'm being blackmailed to kill innocent people."

"And what were you expecting them to do?"

"I have phone records with your buddy Niko. They could've helped trace the calls, maybe narrow down a general area where my mother is being held."

"Your mom is fine," Steele said, his tone patronizing and exasperated. "I don't need to fill you in on what happens if you don't deal with those names on the list. Niko already caught you up to speed."

I knew it. Of course this pathetic excuse of a man is working with Niko.

"Why me?" Danny asked, his brow turning inward. "I'm not even a trained assassin."

Steele finally took his feet off the table and leaned forward, planting his elbows on the surface. "No one on that list requires a trained professional. They're all DEA agents, like you were. We trust your expertise to get close to them and kill them."

Danny needed to test the waters before continuing this conversation. "I saw Zakary Larocque on the list. Is that the same Zak from the D.C. office?"

"I wondered if you'd remember him." Steele laughed. "Everyone on that list is causing problems for my department. They have knowledge of certain activities, which, if shared, will cause serious harm not just to the DEA, but other government agencies."

"And that's my problem?"

Steele tossed his hands up. "It's all our problem, Danny. I have a final offer for you. Five hundred thousand for each name on that list, and we'll make sure nothing ever comes back to you."

Disgust roiled within Danny. "Two and a half million dollars to kill five people? You went from blackmail to bribery. That tells me you're getting desperate. Can't find anyone else to kill these innocent people? Niko won't get off his lazy ass, I presume?"

"I don't need to bribe you, Cortez. I just saved your life. If anything, you owe me."

"Kidnapping me in a van is hardly saving my life. What delusional world do you live in?"

"There are lots of moving parts. If you had entered that FBI office today, I guarantee you'd be dead before tomorrow's sunrise. Sure, you might have gotten lucky and had an agent help you. But word spreads fast. The wrong people would've found out what you were on the verge of uncovering, and they can't have that."

"You're not calling the shots?" Danny refused to look away from Steele, eyes boring into the man's soul.

"I call the shots for the DEA."

"Congratulations on the promotion. They'll choose anyone these days."

"D.C. has always been crawling with incompetent buffoons. Don't group me with the rest of them. My promotion was earned."

Danny snorted, and Steele bit his bottom lip, nostrils flaring. Danny was getting to him. "Sounds like you're not as important as you think. Why else would you be here, meeting with a nobody like me?"

Steele's face soured. "Who have you been messaging?"

"Messaging?"

"Don't play dumb. We went through your phone. Saw the text. You're playing lots of games with burner phones it appears. We'll figure it out eventually. But for now, someone tipped you off about the CIA. Who was it?"

Danny laughed. "I'm not saying a word. You can either kill me today or let me go. If you release my mom, I'll forget any of this and live in peace. And you can keep doing whatever corruption you've fallen into."

"Corruption?" Steele snickered. "I wish I could claim corruption. This is an international crime syndicate, and we're all just pawns in the game. Your friend who told you about the CIA was right. They've been working with cartels across Central and South America. It started with a few shady agents skimming money off their deals with these crooks, but it has snowballed into so much more."

"The CIA? They would never." Danny rolled his eyes.

Steele narrowed his gaze on Danny. "The CIA can do whatever they want. They have their fingers in every department, either through force or bribery. And it all trickles down from there. No one in our government is better equipped to make people disappear than the CIA. If you fall out of line with their orders, you can kiss your ass goodbye."

"You're suggesting the CIA created this list of names for me to remove? They know nothing about me."

"You're getting it now. Of course, they could remove these people themselves, but they want nothing tied back to them. They lean on the different agencies to remove those they deem as threats to their operation. Anyone who might rat them out or have a change of heart. It's not a fun time to work in any agency." He reached into his suit pocket and pulled out a wad of cash, tossing it on the table. "But it's a lucrative time—if you go along."

"So, people are getting rich or getting killed?"

"Precisely. It's a no-brainer. Which side do you want to be on? This is one hundred thousand dollars. It's yours if you agree to proceed with the list. Nothing bad can happen to you. Even if you were caught in the act by a police officer, we have plans in place to help. The CIA owns plenty of judges around the country who have no issues making a 'clerical error' to see your release from prison—if it came to that, of course."

Danny eyed the money. He'd seen that amount of cash before, after busting plenty of drug rings. But never in such a tight bundle, waiting for him to grab. His mind raced for his next move. If this was all a cash grab for those involved, he trusted the whole thing would come crashing down in due time.

Greed always got the best of men. The desire for *more* superseded logic and led to mistakes. That fate awaited these sick, rapacious men.

"How high up does this go?" Danny asked. "It can't stop at the CIA. They have to answer to the White House."

"I don't know for sure," Steele said, "but I imagine it goes all the way to the top. The fun part, Danny, is there's no end in sight. They've made a thorough plan to keep this operation running for years, and the ending will be even better."

"Why would it end?"

Steele laughed. "C'mon, Cortez. The cartels will eventually learn they're getting ripped off. Once that happens, the CIA has plans to turn all of them over to the DEA. Like a gift-wrapped thank you for your cooperation. Basically, once they've milked all the money they can out of a cartel, we get to raid their operations and collect anything outstanding. Round and round we go. So what's it gonna be, Cortez? Are you in or out?"

Danny sighed and rubbed his forehead. "All I want is a life of peace. For my mother, too. I'm sick of being dragged into crap like this. Being a pawn in corrupt people's game. No matter where I hide, something always forces me back into this life I want to escape."

Steele nodded, folding his hands below his chin. "Consider it done. Do this work, and you'll never hear from me again. I have a friend who can get you a villa in Puerto Vallarta. Ever been? Complete this work for me, and I'll personally see to it that you and your mother move there. Quiet days for the rest of your lives."

Danny stood up and rounded the table. If he could strangle Steele and get away with it, he would. He had his doubts. Steele was as corrupt as anyone. But what choice did he have? If he rejected Steele, Danny's days would be filled with constant harassment.

He picked up the hundred thousand, cradled the cash in one arm, and whipped out his hand to shake.

CHAPTER TWELVE

THEY ACTUALLY LET HIM GO.

Danny exchanged fake pleasantries with Steele before leaving the conference room. The deranged administrator believed Danny was on his side. And, more importantly, had zero suspicions about Danny and Zak communicating.

Whatever Zak had done on his end, he covered his trail to perfection.

Steele remained at the warehouse. Richards arranged for Danny's ride back to his truck in downtown Dallas but didn't accompany him. Danny rode in the back of the van alone, the driver partitioned from the rest of the vehicle.

He never glimpsed the driver's face, but the man pounded on the wall and shouted, "Get out!" upon their arrival.

Danny climbed out of the van, his keys and his cell phone restored. When the van sped off, Danny glanced toward the FBI offices and sat in his truck.

Even if I wanted to go in there, I can't now. They'll be watching my every move until I deliver results.

Danny asked Steele for extra time before killing Marcus Vance. He'd explained his desire to carry out the attack his way. Not based on the information Niko had supplied.

Steele reluctantly agreed and promised Danny hell if he didn't follow through.

Sensing he had no time to waste, Danny jammed the key into the ignition and left downtown. He returned to Denton and went straight to Vance's house.

If they're not expecting me to make a move for the next few days, this is my best chance of them not following me.

Danny had devised a plan during the drive back downtown. It would work, but required cooperation from several moving parts. He needed a new burner phone to call Nadia and confirm her help with a portion of the plan. But visiting Vance had top priority right now.

It had been nearly ten hours since Danny had scoped out the neighborhood earlier that morning. Kids played in the street or in their yards. Families strolled the block, enjoying the warm summer evening.

But the Vance family remained inside, all gathered around their dining table.

It's now or never.

Danny parked in the spot across the street and jumped out of his truck, racing up the pathway to the front door. They spotted him through the window, but he rang the doorbell anyway.

Marcus Vance came to the door and cracked it open to peer at Danny. "May I help you?"

"Yes, Mr. Vance, you may not remember me, but you were an instructor of mine at the DEA. I'm Danny Cortez."

Vance pulled the door all the way open, beaming with subtle recognition. "Name sounds familiar, but I'm not quite remembering. Forgive me. I taught over seven hundred new recruits during my time in that role. What brings you to my home?"

Danny checked over his shoulder. No other vehicles had arrived since he parked. "There's a situation, Mr. Vance. Extremely sensitive. Can we speak in private?"

A confused frown replaced Vance's grin as he chewed on his bottom lip. He studied Danny, perhaps seeking any sign of a bluff. But Danny held firm.

"Come in," Vance said, stepping aside to allow room for Danny to pass.

He entered the house, and Vance closed the door.

"Thank you, sir," Danny said. "Mr. Vance, I have very little time, but your life is in danger. Before you jump to conclusions, I have a plan. If you'll hear me out."

"Marcus," his wife called from the dining room. "Who was it?"

Vance glanced back then returned his gaze to Danny.

Danny nodded. "My plan involves your family's cooperation. They should join us."

"An old friend," Vance shouted back. "Sweetie, could you close the curtains in the dining room?"

"The curtains? Why?"

"Just do it, please."

Vance gulped before pulling the curtains in the living room shut. He pivoted and waved Danny to follow him to the dining room.

"We have company," he said. His wife shot a blank stare at Danny, looking back and forth between him and Vance. Their kids had their noses down in their cell phones. "This is Danny Cortez with the DEA. He was a student of mine."

The brief tension lifted. His wife lit up as she circled the table to shake Danny's hand. "Welcome to our home, Danny. I'm Katie. Can I fix you a plate for dinner?"

Danny hadn't eaten since the continental breakfast, but currently had no appetite. "I'll have to pass, but I appreciate it."

"Take a seat, Danny." Vance gestured to the open seat next to his son. "These are our kids, Anthony and Danielle. Phones down, kids."

"Nice to meet you both." Danny slid into the seat and crossed his hands on the table.

"Everyone listen to Mr. Cortez." Vance returned to his seat, where a plate contained remnants of barbecue chicken and vegetables. "Phones!"

The kids stuffed their phones into their pockets, looking back up with bored expressions.

"High schoolers." Vance rolled his eyes.

All heads turned to Danny, who shifted. "First off, I need to ask you, Mr. Vance, why did you welcome me in here with no hesitation?

If someone knocked on my door and said what I told you, I'd slam the door in their face."

Vance chuckled. "If you found me with such ease, that tells me you're working with the government. And claiming my life is in danger confirms some of my suspicions."

"Suspicions? About what?"

"I still have friends in various agencies. I had drinks with an old buddy from the CIA about six months ago. Clark Patton. We caught up on life and all that, but he told me about concerns he had about corruption in his department. Made some wild accusations about other agencies also being involved. It all sounded absurd. A fantasy. But I started digging into things myself. Well, as much as I could with Google."

"And this led to threats on your life?"

"Not directly," Vance said. "But my friend won't talk to me now. Said we needed to stop discussing the matter before someone gets hurt. I never assumed myself, but I've wondered. Then you show up today telling me pretty much the same thing. Even with internal corruption, I always believed that good people would rise to the top. So that leaves one question for you, Mr. Cortez. Regardless of what is or isn't happening, are you with the good guys?"

Danny licked his lips. He never expected this discussion to flow this seamlessly. But he apparently wasn't the only one looking into the corruption.

"I've met the men involved with this scheme," Danny said. "If I wasn't one of the good guys, I'd have shot you when you opened the door."

"Precisely." Vance grinned. "Now, tell me everything."

After catching the Vances up to speed about everything Danny had just learned from Steele, he laid out his plan. All four Vances scooted to the edge of their seats.

"We need to fake your death, Mr. Vance. And all of you will need to go along with it until this entire situation can be resolved."

Katie pressed her hand against her mouth. The kids stared at Danny, bug eyed.

"How do you even fake someone's death?" Katie asked. "What would we have to do?"

"Not much," Danny said. "I have a friend who's helped me do this before. She can forge a death certificate, obituary, anything we need. You all need to disappear, though. To make it most believable, we may need to position Mr. Vance's death as a suicide. Or some sort of accident—maybe a slip in the shower. Attention to detail is everything. All three of you will need to be out of the house and with someone else at the time of Mr. Vance's fake death. The last thing we need are accusations of murder and the investigations that follow."

"That's not a problem," Vance said. He didn't appear bothered by this discussion. Slightly intrigued, in fact. "It's summer break. Why don't the three of you plan a tee time at the country club?"

"That's perfect," Danny said. "Not only does that provide an alibi, there will be records of you three checking in at the golf course, and you'll be seen by other people."

Katie turned pale. "Then what? We come home and pretend to find Marcus dead in the shower?"

"Mr. Vance won't be here." Danny turned his attention to Vance. "That morning, you'll need to leave town. No cell phone or credit cards. Take cash and check into a hotel. Leave your car, wallet, and any belongings behind. I can give you a ride."

"And what are we supposed to do?" Danielle asked. "Pretend to mourn our father's death? Are we going to have a fake funeral and all that, too?"

"You'll need to stick around for a few days and show the community you're grieving. It would definitely look suspicious if you disappeared immediately, even with an alibi. Not everyone has funerals. If anyone asks, just say you're having the body cremated with no service. Lots of ways to play that off. After a week, I'd suggest you come up with a story about needing to get away. And you should. Take a vacation. Go to Mexico for a couple weeks. Just don't stick around here. Eventually, these thugs will come snooping around for proof of his death."

Katie dabbed at tears forming in her eyes. "If they're the government, can't they check systems for his death records?"

"Not necessarily," Danny said. "But if they do, my friend will have that all covered. Wherever they think to look, they'll find proof of his death."

"How can you be so sure?"

"She did this for my mother once." Danny's chest ached at the mention of his mother. He was doing this all for her. "Long story, but I needed to hide her from a cartel. Faking her death was the only way to get them off her trail."

"And these people aren't asking for any sort of proof that Marcus is dead? A picture?"

Danny shrugged. "They haven't mentioned anything about me providing proof. I suppose they don't want any physical evidence floating around out there. I trust they'll take his absence and obituary as enough."

Anthony spoke for the first time. "And when is this all supposed to happen?"

"As soon as possible. They're expecting your father's death within the next five days."

Katie hyperventilated while the kids exchanged worried looks. Vance, however, remained composed. Focused. He stood up to address his family, rubbing a hand on his wife's back.

"We can do this," he said. "I have faith in Mr. Cortez and his plan. If the things I've been researching are indeed true, then we either need to do this, or risk my death becoming a reality." He turned back to look at Danny. "Count me in, Mr. Cortez."

CHAPTER THIRTEEN

ALL HAD GONE SMOOTHLY with the faked death of Marcus Vance. Under Vance's direction, his family booked the tee time two days after Danny had met with them. While they enjoyed a round of golf together, Danny drove a disguised Vance to Houston and dropped him off at the bus station.

Vance had vowed to catch a bus east to Alabama, where he'd hide out until receiving further instruction. They had stopped to each buy burner phones and exchange numbers before departing. Danny stressed that Vance should only call him if he believed his life was in danger.

Danny had called Nadia immediately after leaving Vance and filled her in on everything, confident his new phone would go untracked for at least a few days. Contrary to what he'd done in the past, Danny held on to his old burner phone as a decoy in case Steele and his goons believed that was his real phone. He still wouldn't reach out to Zak, leaving his friend to gauge the risk of their communications.

Nadia had promised to make the proper arrangements, reminding Danny she was only involved until his mother was released.

After making the nearly four-hour drive back to Denton, Danny had locked himself in his hotel room and waited.

The Vances had planned to delay their return home after golf by making a stop for lunch and shopping. When they arrived closer to five o'clock, the plan officially kicked into gear.

Danny didn't know how much acting they planned to do. Would Katie and the kids scream? Tell their neighbors? He doubted it. They weren't the type to blast their business to the world, but they needed to leak the fake news to at least a few sources.

The following morning, Danny received a text message from Steele, congratulating him on a job well done and requesting a private meeting.

Danny opened the Denton News on his phone to see the story of Marcus Vance's death covered in a brief article. Short and simple, with the stroke of genius he expected from Nadia.

She hit all the points to keep the story under wraps without giving any suspicions. Family was away while Vance stayed home ill. Vance had an accident and slipped in the shower. Died instantly. Brief information about Vance's past with the DEA. Family requesting privacy during this sensitive time.

Danny grinned as he read the article and responded to Steele.

Where are we meeting?

He dressed for the day ahead and ran downstairs to grab a muffin and toast for breakfast. When he returned to his room, Steele had responded.

STEELE

Same place. Van will pick you up in ten minutes. Be ready.

Danny rolled his eyes and headed back to the lobby to wait. When the van arrived, they went through the same routine as last time, although not as rough.

When he arrived at the warehouse, a security team greeted him with a pat-down, taking his cell phone—the old burner they recognized. He'd loved to have brought his Glock, but didn't trust these men to give it back when he left.

"There's the man of the hour!" Steele stepped out from the nearest office with his arms raised high, a wide smile plastered across his face. Another man followed behind him as they approached Danny. Steele shook Danny's hand before throwing an arm around him and hugging like they were old pals. "I didn't think you had it in you, Cortez. I'm impressed. And making it look like an accident in the shower. Pure genius! You keep this up, and we'll have a permanent job for you."

Danny forced a grin of pride. "Thank you, sir. Nothing much to it. Just waited for the family to get out of the house and took care of business."

Steele cackled and slapped Danny on the back. "So modest. You gotta give me more than that. Did he cry? Scream like a girl? How'd he go out?"

Danny debated saying nothing and leaning further into the "modest" approach. But he needed to keep stringing Steele along if he planned to turn him in one day. "He never saw me coming. Had no chance to react. When his head hit the shower wall, I wasn't sure if the sound was his skull or the porcelain cracking."

Steele howled with glee, still slapping Danny on the back. "You're too much, Cortez. You *actually* killed him in the shower?"

"Easiest place to wash all the evidence down the drain."

"I never knew you had such a dog living inside you. Welcome to the team, Cortez. We're glad to have you."

Danny faked another grin before turning to the man who had tagged along with Steele.

"Where are my manners?" Steele said. "Cortez, this is Clark Patton. He works with the CIA and has been helping us out as a liaison between our people and their people. Lots of moving parts."

Danny's stomach knotted. *The same Clark Patton Vance had just mentioned a couple of days ago?*

Danny didn't want to believe it, but how many Clark Pattons could work for the CIA? And have connections to all of this?

"Nice to meet you, Clark." Danny stuck out his hand.

Clark studied it before returning the shake, sneering as though Danny hadn't washed his hands in a week. He squeezed and dug his thumb into the flesh between Danny's index finger and thumb. "Pleasure's all mine."

They let go, and Clark glared at Danny. Vengeance filled Clark's eyes, and every ounce of that rage radiated across the room. In a warehouse with no rules, he just might kill Danny without a worry of consequences.

He thinks I killed his friend. I have to get him alone and tell him the truth.

"Shall we?" Steele said, clapping them both on the back. "Let's head to my office. We have business to discuss."

The two men followed Steele toward his office, ignoring the dozens of others moving around the warehouse, going about whatever absurd tasks Steele had saddled them with.

They entered the first office, and Steele closed the door behind them. He had a desk along the wall, two file cabinets behind his chair, and a plant leaning in the corner. The frosted windows provided no view of the rest of the warehouse.

"Have a seat, gentlemen." Steele rounded his desk and reached under it while Danny and Clark got situated. Steele pulled out a black duffel bag and plopped it on the desk, pushing it toward Danny. "Five hundred thousand dollars for the death of Marcus Vance. Seeing how clean the job was, I'll see about adding in a few more after your next job."

Danny caught Clark out of the corner of his eye. The man hadn't looked away from him since they shook hands.

"Thank you, sir." Danny pulled the bag towards himself and rested it on his lap.

Dirty money. The Vances deserve every penny for having to go through this.

Steele's phone buzzed on his desk. After checking it, he rolled his head back. "Excuse me for a moment, gentlemen. I need a couple of minutes to deal with something outside."

Steele exited the office without another word and left Danny enclosed in a room with a man who clearly wanted to murder him.

Danny immediately raised a finger to his lips. He scanned the room for any visible cameras or bugs. When he spotted none, he whispered just loud enough for Clark to hear. "Vance isn't dead. I know who you are. He told me about you."

Clark's glare softened, but his eyes remained fixed on Danny.

Studying him. Picking apart his words. Why should Clark trust this guy Steele praised and adored?

Clark finally glanced away, dropping his stare to the floor. He whispered back, "He better be alive."

"The family is all in on it. I promise he's safe. Dropped him off in Houston myself."

Footsteps approached from outside the office and the two men fell silent. Danny breathed easier, knowing Clark wouldn't jam the pair of scissors on Steele's desk through his eyeball. CIA guys could turn anything into a lethal weapon.

The door swung open, and Steele returned to the seat behind his desk, clasping his hands together. "Sorry about that, gentlemen. I've mentioned we have lots of moving parts in this operation. With that comes lots of problems to address. People like to find their conscience and get cute. Can you believe it?"

Danny's heart drummed. Steele's tone had gone from friendly to accusatory.

This office is bugged. He heard everything I just said. Guess I'm getting killed either way.

"I'm not gonna sit here and preach about loyalty," Steele continued. "Loyalty is for kings. What I want is trust. I trust you, and you trust me. That's how we all take care of each other. Once that trust is broken, however, it can't ever be repaired."

Danny gulped. This was it. Bullet incoming between his eyes. Dying in a place he didn't even know. What a pathetic excuse for an ending.

But Steele didn't look at Danny. He drew circles on his desk with his finger.

"Isn't that right, Clarky boy?" Steele said.

In a flash, Steele yanked open his desk drawer, pulled out a Beretta, and shot Clark in the head.

CHAPTER FOURTEEN

CLARK TIPPED BACK in his seat and hit the floor with a heavy thud.

His limbs splayed out in every direction, eyes glossy as they gazed emptily at the flickering fluorescent light in the ceiling.

"Sorry you had to see that." Steele tucked the pistol back into the desk drawer. "Messy business. Part of the job."

Danny swallowed down the lump that had formed in his throat, fighting away the quiver creeping into his arms. He glanced over his shoulder at the dead Clark, the urge to vomit rising in his stomach as the metallic stench of blood filled the room. He held his breath for the next several seconds, focused on keeping his sanity in one piece.

Steele pulled out his phone and dialed, pressing it against his ear. "Hey. Yes. It was Patton. Arrange for the cleaners in about thirty minutes." He hung up and leaned back in his seat like nothing had happened. "My friend here was working as a double agent of sorts. The CIA and DEA have been cooperating on this project, so naturally there's overlap. We do strict vetting before letting anyone in. Patton here has been collecting notes on both of our departments and made plans to share his findings with the press. Everyone wants to be the hero until they catch a bullet in the head, right?"

Steele giggled. The room spun around Danny. "Right, sir." He forced the words out and hoped they didn't sound too shaky.

"Anyway, where were we?" Steele glanced at the duffel bag of money and nodded. "Ah, yes. Your mother. After how successfully your first assassination went, I thought it was only fair to share an update about your mom."

Steele opened the laptop resting on his desk and twiddled his fingers while it powered on. He entered his password and clicked around for a few moments before spinning the laptop around to Danny.

The screen showed his mother sitting in her wheelchair in a makeshift bedroom. The concrete flooring suggested another warehouse. Could she possibly be in the same building as them?

The room had a bed, a nightstand, and a TV mounted on the wall. It also came with medical equipment. A ventilator, EKG machine, and patient monitor. She wasn't connected to any of them.

Danny narrowed his eyes on the screen, searching for clues of where she might be, or what condition she was in.

She appeared fine, stationary in her chair while watching an episode of *Wheel of Fortune*.

"See," Steele said. "Your mom is alive and well. I spoke with the crew this morning for an update on her health, and they said she's doing fine. Don't mind all the hospital equipment. That's there just in case. She hasn't needed anything besides her routine medications."

Seeing his mother gave Danny hope. These people were monsters, sure, but they'd kept her as comfortable as possible, considering the situation.

"Has she been eating?" Danny asked. "Her appetite is hit or miss with her medication."

Steele shrugged. "I didn't get into details. They only told me there have been no complications, and they've rather enjoyed her company." He turned the laptop back around, and Danny almost pleaded for more time.

"Why did you show her to me?"

Steele closed the laptop and clasped his hands together on top of it. "As a token of good faith. With your first assassination complete, I took that as a sign of faith from *you*. I'm simply returning the favor. It's easier to work when we know our loved ones are taken care of.

Complete your next four assassinations, and your mother will be released to you immediately."

Danny licked his lips before responding. "Mr. Steele. When I'm done with this list, you know I have no plans to continue with any of this. I'll have enough money to live my life in peace, and plan to do just that."

"I understand. I'd still like to have a conversation with you when the jobs are all complete. Maybe we can find a reduced role for you. Certainly, no more killing. But you're too sharp a guy to let walk away completely."

"I'm open to a conversation," Danny said, "but my mind is fairly set. I might leave the country altogether. Start over elsewhere with a clean slate."

"And I respect that. We'll talk. Just keep up the good work." Steele glanced at the dead body on the floor, his mouth curled in disgust. "Now, the next name on your list is Eva Ramirez. She lives in D.C. and was recently fired by the CIA. The official reason is listed as insubordination, but she was merely getting too close to uncovering our operations. Naturally, she needs to be eliminated before she can speak to anyone about her findings."

"When was she fired?"

"Two days ago. Why does that matter?"

"Good to know what I'm dealing with. She'll be in plenty of distress right now. Could be the prime opportunity to make a move."

Steele slapped the top of his desk, startling Danny, who remained on edge thanks to the dead body lying three feet to his right. "One down and ready to jump right back into the next one. My kinda guy. No waiting or resting. Just get the work done. When do you want to head east?"

"Excuse me?"

"You're in now, Cortez. No more driving across the country in that busted truck of yours. We can arrange flights, hotels, rental cars. Just let us know what you need."

Danny hated when people dissed his truck. It was his baby. Few things got under his skin, but harsh words toward his Tundra set him off. He brushed his flash of anger aside. "I can leave immediately. Just need to stop at the hotel in Denton first. Still have some things to grab. I can't take my gun with me to the airport. What should I do with it? And my truck?"

"You'll be flying private with our guys. You can take whatever you need. No airport. Private hangar. As for your truck, where would you like it delivered? Leave the keys in the glove compartment, and I'll have someone drive it wherever you'd like. Even back to Colorado."

Danny had never received such red-carpet treatment in his life and didn't know how to approach it. "Can I just drive to D.C.? I'm not a fan of flying."

Steele frowned. "Okay. That's your call, but the option is available. I'd recommend stashing your truck when you arrive and using a rental we can provide. Just to be safe."

"That's fine. My truck feels like home. It's only twenty hours from here to Washington. I'll be there in two days."

Steele rose from his seat and extended his hand. "It's been a pleasure, and I look forward to your continued work. Safe travels. And I'll see you out there."

They exchanged more small talk before Steele let him go. After stepping around Clark's body, Danny rushed into the warehouse where the van waited to take him back to his hotel in Denton.

Another quiet ride in solitude, but his mind raced with the possibilities of the future. Could he pull off more fake deaths? He got lucky with Vance, who was eager to play along—as was his family. Not everyone would be so trusting. Or even believe what Danny had to say.

Zak would certainly go along with the ploy, but the other two were wild cards.

Thirty minutes later, Danny arrived back at the hotel and returned to his room to pack his belongings before hitting the road. He had locked his new burner phone in the room's safe and found dozens of missed text messages.

All messages came from the same number. Vance's number.

VANCE

My friend has proof of Steele's involvement.
Lots of it.

He's going to share it with the press.

Major bombshell coming to Washington.

They'll never see it coming.

Danny's heart dropped. Attachments and downloadable links accompanied these messages. Danny downloaded them all before they expired but didn't open them yet. Vance was out of control. He wasn't supposed to keep digging into this matter while hiding away after his fake death.

Danny called Vance, pacing circles around the room while he waited for him to pick up.

"Danny?" Vance answered. "Is it done already?"

"I told you to not to contact me unless your life is in danger," Danny replied through gritted teeth. "These guys have eyes all over the government. Clark is dead. I watched him get shot in the head. They knew he was going to leak his findings."

"But—"

"Shut up and listen. You need to stop whatever research you're doing and completely unplug from this whole situation. No Google. Nothing. Go buy a different burner phone and send me a fake spam message so I know it's you. Then destroy the phone you're on right now."

"But Danny—"

"No. We cannot speak until this is done. Break the phone with a hammer and toss it down a storm drain. We can't take any chances. Are we clear?"

"Yes, Danny. I'm sorry. I just thought this could end sooner if this info was shared."

"That's what Clark thought, too. And now he's dead." Silence settled between the men. "Back off," Danny said, "or they'll kill us both."

CHAPTER FIFTEEN

DANNY DROVE ten hours and stayed at a motel in Nashville, roughly the halfway mark between Dallas and D.C.

He arrived at ten o'clock at night and checked in, intent on sleeping the rest of the night away.

But he couldn't. Not with the handful of attachments Vance had sent him. They were already on his phone, so he figured reviewing them could only help.

Vance never explained how he'd come across any of the information he'd compiled, aside from claiming to use Google. But the level of detail made Danny doubt that. He didn't know exactly what Vance used to do for the CIA, but presumed it involved hacking technology. Nothing else explained what Danny opened and read.

Phone logs, text message chains, and emails between different departments of the U.S. government. Every agency had a contact within the communications, along with members from foreign governments, all Central and South American. Honduras, Panama, Mexico, Colombia, Peru and Ecuador.

Across five different attachments, Danny found fifty pages of material to review. Vance presented his findings like a book, beginning with the addition of Charles Steele inside the DEA. Steele had been an FBI academy reject and somehow landed a role as an entry-level data analyst in the DEA many years before his eventual rise to deputy administrator, where he worked as the number two in the agency.

From there, plans kicked into action to remove the administrator, Alice Mildred. A smear campaign was on the verge of being launched to accuse Mildred of drinking on the job and harassing the interns—who were hired strictly to give false testimony against Mildred.

They scrapped the plan when a post in the president's cabinet opened and forced Mildred through a prompt confirmation hearing. Having the administrator promoted rather than removed by scandal cleared a smoother path for Steele to fill her role.

The plan worked, and Steele now oversaw the DEA after passing his own confirmation hearing three weeks after Mildred departed for the White House.

And that was only the DEA. Similar actions had occurred at the other agencies. Heads of departments were replaced for what appeared as valid reasons to the public. But all moves were done with a corrupt future in mind.

New staff replaced lifelong employees. Shifts occurred in communications systems. Vance had receipts of every little detail that made the corruption possible. As Danny flipped through the research, his curiosity grew. The coordination required someone to make all the decisions and see the implementations through. The final five pages brought everything into focus.

Overseeing the entire scheme was Richard Calloway, the junior senator representing Louisiana. Vance tied everything to him through a series of text messages and emails. Calloway had communicated with each department at different times, all regarding the changes of leadership. Calloway vowed to get support in the senate for the upcoming nominees and had arranged events where his preferred nominees could brush shoulders with those senators whose votes they would eventually need.

Steele had attended an event nearly ten years ago, when he was still a data analyst with the DEA. Not a role that typically warranted such an invitation, but Calloway got his people in the right rooms to shake hands and build bonds.

It took a decade for the plan to come to fruition, and Calloway never wavered from his vision. His biggest feat was covering his tracks. Even with the story Vance had beautifully outlined, not a shred of evidence could be traced back to the senator.

His emails to Steele were done through official government accounts and discussed nothing illegal. His texts to the head of the CIA were all business. While nothing was discussed directly regarding their scheme, the moves all added up.

It would take an extensive, and possibly forensic, approach to pin any of this on Calloway. Even with Vance's virtual playbook of facts, the lines still had to be drawn directly to Calloway.

A crooked senator probably has a few people ready to take the fall. Especially one this good at covering their tracks.

Danny wished he could tell Vance to keep digging, but that would only endanger the man's life. The push would need to come from the outside. If a lone senator could wield so much influence over independent government agencies, no one within the government could actually be trusted if confronted with this information.

He pulled out his cell phone and dialed Nadia, despite it being almost midnight for her in Chicago.

She answered, her voice wide awake. "Danny?"

"How'd you know it was me?"

She sighed. "Who else would call from a weird number in the middle of the night?"

"Fair point," he said. "You can save this as my new burner number."

"Of course. What's so pressing that couldn't wait until the morning?"

"The better question is, why are you still awake? Don't you have court in the morning?"

"Sure do, but there's never enough time in the day to complete all the paperwork that piles up. I was just about to wrap up and call it a night."

"Well, I'm glad you answered."

"Did everything go smoothly with the plan I helped execute?"

"Yes. Our guy is hiding in a different state, and the crooked feds don't think anything different. They bought all of it." Danny yawned, the long day on the road catching up with him. "I suppose I owe you a thank you."

Nadia giggled, sounding rather slap-happy. "Let me guess, it's time for the next one. You said there's a list."

"Soon enough, and I'll be in touch about that. For now, I've come across something that could bring the whole thing down. No further faking of deaths required."

He explained everything Vance had sent over, concluding with the strong probability Senator Calloway had been the brains behind this operation for nearly ten years.

"He sure sounds patient and calculated," Nadia said. "If it was anything else, you might call him dedicated and resilient."

"We can absolutely call him that. Those words aren't reserved for people who do good things. Calloway might be the hardest working senator nobody talks about. He votes in line with his party, fights for his state, sits on a committee for children's cancer research, and has worked across the aisle on several bills. Judging by all appearances, and his sixty-four percent approval rating, no one would question that this senator has carried out his job to near perfection."

"And what do you want me to do?" Nadia asked. "I can't just sue a senator out of the blue. That would get me in so much hot water."

"Never that," Danny said. "I want you to leak this story to the press. I'm sure you have some trustworthy connections who'll take this seriously. It's gonna be a mess to investigate, but the right reporter can bring all of this to light. And when that happens, Calloway's criminal empire will collapse on itself. What do you think? You can even do it anonymously. No reason for your name to be tied to anything."

"And you're sure this Vance guy is legit. This isn't some kind of twisted joke to lead you down the wrong path. What if he's been compromised?"

Danny jerked his head from side to side. "Not Vance. He may not be a friend, but I trust him. And we don't really have a choice."

Nadia was silent for a moment. "I don't know, Danny. This seems like lighting a match on something and running away."

"Exactly. Neither of us needs to see what happens. Hell, we don't even know if it will lead to anything. But we need to get the word out there. The press can launch a story, start investigations, and maybe get his voters to press him for answers. It's worth it just to see how he reacts to the accusations, especially if he's blindsided by them. These guys always think they can get away with it until the day they're headed to prison. A simple leak to the press can lead to justice. Isn't that what you're in the business of?"

"You don't need to sell me, Danny. Just give me a moment to think. Unlike you, I prefer to weigh the pros and cons before committing to anything."

Danny sighed and gave Nadia her moment of silence. She was like this even during their relationship. If they got into an argument, she'd call a timeout to gather her thoughts. This left Danny fuming at times, then Nadia would end the argument with her well-crafted responses, which further enraged Danny.

If she agreed, Danny would have more leverage when convincing others to fake their deaths. With Steele responding with glee to Danny's quick actions, the sooner they leaked the story, the sooner all those involved would burn in the boiling water circling them.

"Okay, Danny," Nadia said. "Send me the files."

CHAPTER SIXTEEN

DANNY GOT A LATE START the next morning, which resulted in his arrival in D.C. at eight o'clock in the evening.

A text from Steele gave details about hotel and rental car reservations. Both had been scheduled for a week with an option to extend if necessary.

Steele had booked him a room at the five-star Washington Hotel one block away from the White House. Danny had never stayed in such an upscale hotel and admired its beauty as he circled the block in search of the parking garage.

The stone facade towered eight stories tall, with an adjoining courtyard illuminated by several strings of lights hanging from tree to tree.

Danny found the garage entrance and drove his truck underground. If he had to hide his truck, underground was always the best option. No risk of random tickets or thieves.

He parked, the hot engine ticking as it cooled after the excruciating drive from Nashville had led him through two thunderstorms and gusts of wind that surprisingly never became tornadoes.

Danny snatched his duffel bag and headed for the elevator, locking his truck behind him. Much cooler than the outside world, he enjoyed the climate in the garage. Being on Steele's dime, he looked forward to blasting the A/C as hard as he pleased in his room.

He rode the elevator up to the main lobby. Checkered marble

flooring led to the front desk. Danny joined the short line of patrons waiting to check in. White walls with gold trim surrounded him. Gaudy chandeliers hung from the ceiling, their dangling jewels sparkling in the light. Soft jazz poured out from the nearby hotel bar, where men and women in formal attire clinked their glasses and babbled the night away.

"Excuse me, sir?" a voice called, shaking Danny out of his daydream. The man behind the front desk welcomed Danny with a warm smile. "Are you checking in?"

"Yes." Danny lunged forward and rested his arms on the countertop—also made of marble. "Reservation under Daniel Cortez."

"May I see an ID, please?"

Danny slid his ID across the counter and continued to glance around the hotel lobby. Sofas and lounge chairs filled the area, mostly occupied by people who found a quiet refuge away from the bar to carry on their conversations.

There were also men in black suits and sunglasses peppered throughout the lobby. They had blended in at first, but Danny recognized them the second time around.

Secret Service? Could be a higher-up senator somewhere in the hotel.

As one of them locked eyes with him, Danny turned back around to face the hotel clerk. The agent's gaze burned into his back.

You're just paranoid. There are eyes all over this city. And that's why you're not going to kill anyone in Washington.

Danny had toyed around with ideas for faking Eva's death but couldn't set anything in stone until he had a sense of her routine and living situation. If she had been recently fired, missing work was no longer a complication. Did she have regular contact with family or friends? All bases needed covering before proceeding with anything.

The clerk frowned as he studied his screen. "It appears your partner has already checked in."

Danny almost asked what the hell he was talking about but bit his tongue. "I wasn't aware they were already here. Can I get my own room keys?"

"Certainly. One moment."

Danny's thoughts raced almost as fast as his heart. Who the hell had checked into his room?

"Room 724." The clerk pushed the miniature envelope with key cards across the counter along with Danny's ID. "Elevator will take you right up. Please let us know if you need anything during your stay and enjoy your time in Washington."

Danny nodded at the clerk, grabbed his cards, and moved away from the counter. He pulled out his old burner phone that Steele had used to communicate with him and sent a text message.

Is someone staying in my room with me?

He waited two minutes and received no response. The men in black suits remained unchanged in their positions.

"Are you guys watching me?" Danny whispered under his breath. His leg bounced as his impatience elevated. He sent another text message to Steele.

???????

After another minute passed, he dialed Steele's number. The call went to voicemail after six rings.

Danny's senses heightened. Steele wouldn't have booked the same room for someone else and not mentioned it. The chattering voices from the bar grew louder. The front desk's phone rang, loud as a siren. And through all the commotion and noise, those men—he had counted four—remained statues. All staring in the same direction—the front desk—looking nowhere else.

Danny slung his bag over his shoulder and hurried to the elevators. No one else was in the vicinity, and when the doors parted, he stepped in and tapped the button to close the doors ten times in rapid succession. He checked the upper corners of the elevator.

No cameras.

The doors closed, and he dropped to a knee, rummaging through his bag for his Glock. He reached blindly, letting his fingers flail around while he monitored the ascending floor numbers. When it reached six, he found the gun and yanked it out from the messy pile of clothes that had buried it. He shoved it into his waistband before the doors opened.

The elevator stopped and chimed to welcome him to the seventh floor. The doors parted to a small lobby just as gaudy as the main one. Two hallways parted in opposite directions, the range of room numbers posted on a sign with arrows directing traffic.

The hallway to his left had rooms 700 through 724.

His paranoia kicked up a notch. A supposed "partner" had already checked in. And the room waited at the end of a long hallway. At least there weren't any men in suits watching him on the seventh floor.

He checked his phone for any response from Steele, saw none, and marched down the lengthy hallway. Glock in hand, he arrived at the door for room 724 and silently placed his bag on the floor.

If someone was in his room, did they know Danny had just checked in? Or had they spent their entire time inside, waiting for him at the peephole?

The logical side of his mind believed it all could have been a clerical mistake. The room was double booked, and the clerk didn't recognize that in the confusion. But nothing about the situation involving Steele had logic. That ship had long sailed.

Do I knock or barge in?

Danny considered his options. If he knocked, he could hide to the side of the door and wait to see who opened it. Or they might not open the door at all, which would only leave them alerted to Danny's potential presence.

Barging in made more sense. But what would he barge into?

If the person in the room *was* expecting Danny, what did they want from him?

This has got to be a setup.

Steele hadn't mentioned anyone else working with him on the assassination of Eva Ramirez. Could it be someone trying to bring down the criminal operation? Surely, Danny and Vance weren't the only two people with hunches about the mass corruption spreading across all the government agencies.

If Vance had dug out the level of detail as a retired CIA agent, what could an active-duty agent uncover? They would likely know about Danny's involvement by now, especially if they had eyes on Steele's lines of communication. They could have intercepted the hotel reservation and arrived at the room first.

Would they know Danny wasn't actually working for the bad guys? Only giving appearances? If they believed otherwise, would they give Danny a moment to explain himself? Or was this a shoot first, ask questions later scenario?

All these thoughts rushed through his mind as the Glock and key card wavered in Danny's hands. He needed to act fast before someone wandered down the hallway and spotted him.

The peephole on the door had remained black the entire time. Either someone was standing in front of it, or the lights inside were all turned off.

Danny held his breath and reached out for the door handle with his gun hand. He tapped the key card, and the moment it beeped and flashed a green light, he jammed the handle down with his palm and shoved his shoulder into the door.

It banged against the wall with a crash, but a louder explosion washed out the sound. The air next to Danny's ear rushed as a bullet whizzed by and planted into the wall behind him.

The door glided shut, and Danny broke into a sprint down the hallway.

CHAPTER SEVENTEEN

DANNY BARRELED DOWN THE HALLWAY, feet moving faster than his mind could process.

He stumbled before reaching the elevator lobby, crashing into the wall, and used the opportunity to look back.

A man dressed in all black, including a balaclava to cover his face, raced after him.

No more elevator.

Danny got to his feet and darted down the other hallway for rooms 725 through 750. The exit sign at the end glowed a bright green. His lungs burned after the mad dash. When he reached the end of the hallway, he spotted a fire alarm and pulled the handle.

Sirens blaring, he kicked open the door to the stairwell and flew down the steps, skipping several at a time. He rolled his ankle a couple of times, adrenaline pulsing through his body and shielding him from the pain.

By the time he reached the landing on the fifth floor, the door from the seventh banged open, followed by manic shouting from above. The U-shaped stairwell allowed the man above to peek over the ledge and fire his gun downward. Danny kept descending the circular steps, dodging each bullet.

"Dammit!" the man shouted. His footsteps pounded on the concrete stairs as he chased after Danny.

Ten seconds later, others poured into the stairwell, most of them begrudgingly. A few were in bathrobes, others in pajamas and appearing groggy. The alarms screeched in maddening echoes off the concrete walls.

None expected to witness a masked gunman chasing after another man with a Glock in hand.

People spilled into the stairwell from each floor, crowding the area and making it impossible for the man to fire any more shots. Unless he didn't care about harming innocent bystanders.

By the time Danny reached the bottom landing of the main lobby, his lungs and legs tingling in protest, at least one hundred people had filed into the stairwell. The ruckus grew deafening, the echoes of those combined panicked voices bouncing off the walls. But no more shots came.

Danny waited at the door for others to catch up to him. He couldn't step out first, not if those men in suits were there for him. A handful of people reached the door and shouted profanities at Danny to get out of the way.

He obliged and shuffled aside, waiting as a group of fifteen more people trudged to the door without a worry in the world. How could these people stay so calm with the fire alarm blaring?

A few children cried while others shrieked, but the mass panic Danny had hoped to spark by pulling the fire alarm never came to fruition. He'd imagined everyone pushing and shoving in a panic, acting selfish. Still, enough people were present to get Danny safely out of the staircase and, hopefully, the building.

The large group reached the door, and Danny shoved his way into the middle. He caught a few elbows and more profanities from those he'd pushed past, but the herd moved with a mind of its own, sweeping him out of the stairwell and into the main lobby.

Sure enough, two men in black suits waited, guns ready. Danny had crouched low enough to remain hidden, but he glimpsed their sunglasses as the group forced their way through the door.

The alarms didn't sound on the main floor, but the lights strobed from their positions high on the walls.

"Please don't panic!" the desk clerk shouted. "We have no reports of a fire. Probably just a kid pulling a prank."

But a crowd filled the lobby area from both the stairwell and the bar. The hum of excited chatter drowned out the man's voice.

Danny kept low and followed a dissipating group exiting the front doors. He stepped out, fresh air hitting his face. But the crowd spread in different directions, leaving Danny exposed.

That's where he encountered the other two men in black suits. One was bald with a beefy neck. The other lanky with slicked back hair. The bald man spotted Danny first and shouted, "Hey! Hands up!"

The man raised his gun, but Danny had spotted him first. He whipped his Glock clean across the side of the man's head, leaving a gash and sending him sprawling to the ground. His tall colleague jerked his gun from his waistband and aimed at Danny.

Danny had no time to respond with anything besides a sloppy lunge toward the man. He wrapped his arms around his scrawny knees, driving his shoulder into the man's pelvis and tackling him to the ground.

Once on the ground, Danny balled a fist and punched the man square in the groin. He yelped, his gun flying as his hands flailed toward his crotch.

A woman shrieked at the unfolding scene, and Danny peered over his shoulder to discover her standing with both hands over her mouth. A group of five people had formed a small huddle around Danny and this suited man, everyone but the woman with their phones out to record the scene.

"Really?" Danny said to the crowd.

He climbed to his feet and kicked the man in the head, ensuring he stayed knocked out. His partner remained along the hotel entrance, stirring, but showing no signs of a fight.

Danny dashed to the garage ramp and ran down it. With those two men taken care of, he could escape the hotel entirely. The other men inside were likely ordered to stay in their positions and wait for Danny to exit the stairwell with everyone else.

The ramp's slope nearly made him fall, but Danny slowed enough to prevent that. He peeked over his shoulder to make sure none of the self-designated paparazzi had followed him.

The garage was silent, and the man working the booth nodded off with a magazine splayed across his lap. He never noticed Danny sprint by and turn left down the first row until reaching his truck.

Danny jumped in, backed out, and skidded toward the exit. His screeching tires startled the parking attendant out of his nap. Danny rolled down his window and tossed a twenty-dollar bill at the man. "Sorry, sir, I'm in a serious rush."

The attendant gawked at the twenty and back to Danny. "Don't you want your change?"

"No, just let me out of here before I break your gate."

The attendant raised his hands and pushed the button to raise the gate arm. Danny sped out of the garage, slamming on his brakes again when he reached the street level. Despite the mayhem unfolding within the hotel, the outside remained fairly empty. Mainly because the people who were outside all gathered around the two unconscious men lying on the pavement.

"Hey!" a man shouted from the group, pointing at Danny. "That's him!"

Danny floored the accelerator, peeling out, the tires sent smoke into the night sky. His truck rolled onto the street, and he vanished without another trace. It was only a matter of time before they'd pull camera footage, and the local authorities would have his plates in their system.

Danny sped but obeyed all red lights and stop signs. Once he reached the outskirts of the nation's capital, he pulled into a McDonald's parking lot to catch his breath.

Adrenaline had been pumping for the last twenty minutes. He could've killed those two men in suits, whoever they were. But that would guarantee his face would be plastered on every television screen in the country.

Danny still had his two phones in his pockets, having left only his clothes behind in the duffel bag at the hotel, along with all that cash. He dialed Steele, begging the universe to make him answer.

"The job is done?" Steele answered.

Rage filled Danny's body, and he squeezed the phone against his ear. "You thought you could kill me in the hotel?"

"Cortez?" Authentic surprise filled Steele's voice. "How—where are you?"

"I'm alive, asshole. Your men couldn't get the job done. You thought you could outsmart me with an assassin in my hotel room and his goons waiting in the lobby? I noticed them before I even checked in."

"We know about the files you read." Steele's surprise vanished as immediately as it had arrived, replaced with a smug, condescending tone. "Who sent those to you? Who are you working with?"

Still doesn't know Vance is alive. A good thing.

"Why would I tell you?" Danny asked, matching the other man's tone. "Getting nervous, Chuck?"

"Nervous?" Steele laughed. "Never. You're the one making mistakes. You expect to walk into a government building with these files and make something happen? Do you know how absurd they will think you are? Or that anyone will take your girlfriend seriously if she leaks this to the press? That won't be happening. I already have men on their way to pick her up. And we might not be so kind this time around."

"Don't you dare."

"It's already in motion. You made the mistake, Cortez. All you had to do was play along. Fill your role and responsibilities. Now you're one of our targets. The biggest target, in fact. We won't rest until you're tossed to the bottom of the Potomac."

CHAPTER EIGHTEEN

AFTER LETTING matters cool off and checking the radio for any news updates about the fiasco at Hotel Washington—there were none —Danny drove west to the city of Annandale, Virginia. He sent Nadia a text, informing her to remain alert and to not go anywhere alone.

I'll call you in a few minutes.

Danny knew the area well, considering his friend Zak lived there. He'd spent plenty of evenings after work at Zak's place, watching sports together and having a few beers.

He drove straight to his friend's neighborhood and parked two blocks away from his house. Danny used his new burner phone to call Nadia, heart racing as it rang.

"Pick up," he muttered to himself. "Pick up."

"Danny?" she answered in a hushed tone. "Danny, what's going on?"

The tension in his shoulders released at the sound of her voice. "Nadia. Are you safe? Where are you?"

"I'm driving around Chicago, hiding. Someone started following me when I left for work. Drove like a maniac through some crowded streets, but I think I lost the car. Haven't seen it in about twenty minutes now. Does this have something to do with you?"

"Yes."

Danny filled her in on everything that had just happened at the hotel, including the whooping he laid on those two men waiting for him outside.

"You've become quite the rebel, Danny. No wonder there's a target on your back."

"You need to leave Chicago. Right now. Come to D.C. It's a two-hour flight. You should be safe going into an airport. I can keep you safe here."

"Danny, I can't just leave—"

"What day is it?"

"Friday."

"It's not safe to go to your house tonight. Let them think you've fled town. Come to D.C. for the weekend. Bring whatever work you need. I'm going to Zak right now to tell him all that's happened. If you hurry, you'll catch a red eye and can be here tonight. I'll pick you up from the airport." Danny stopped, catching himself speaking much too rapidly. "If everything goes well this weekend, I can drive to Chicago and meet you back there. You can land late Sunday night, and I'll check your house to make sure it's safe."

Nadia paused for a moment. "Who's after me, Danny? Steele?"

"Not him personally, but his people. He found out about the files and mentioned you. Said I'm their number one target now, and by extension, that puts you at elevated risk."

"And your mom?"

"They have her. Confirmed. He showed me a video of the room they're keeping her in. So far, she's been fine, but who knows what they have planned now that I've pissed them off. All that aside, you're in danger if you stay put, Nadia. Come to D.C. You and Zak can help me end this without putting yourself in danger."

She scoffed. "Wow, what a tempting offer for a weekend getaway."

"This is serious," Danny said, raking a hand through his hair. "Please consider it."

"I'm on my way to the airport, Danny. Don't need any more motivation than the creep who was following me. I'll call you when I know what flight I'm on and what time I'll be landing."

"Thank God."

"I have nothing but the work clothes on my back. You better have time to take me shopping."

"Of course. Be safe, Nadia. And I'll see you soon."

They hung up, and those last words sent a flutter through Danny's chest. This entire situation was a disaster, but just knowing he'd get to see Nadia in the flesh for the first time in years made it all a little better.

He stepped out of his truck and walked the two blocks to Zak's house, not wanting to risk anyone seeing his vehicle parked out front. Crickets chirped as the humidity stuck to Danny's skin.

Danny moved with an anxious pace, both excited to see his friend and terrified of what trouble they could end up in.

Danny reached Rosewood Street and turned the corner, breaking into a jog when he spotted Zak's house at the end of the block. All the lights were off in the house, but a glow from the television in the living room indicated his friend was home.

Danny trudged up the short walkway to the front door and lowered his face to the camera doorbell. He pressed the button and waved at the camera.

The doorbell chimed inside, and Danny took a step back, placing his hands on his hips.

Seconds later, the door creaked open, a startled Zak peering through the crack in the doorway. "Danny? Is it really you?"

"Hello, my friend." Danny grinned, the dangers of his life fading for a moment. Seeing Zak made him feel at home.

The door opened all the way, revealing Zak's hanging jaw. "You're here. Why?"

Zak stepped outside, dressed in his tattered gym shorts and t-shirt that served as pajamas.

Probably the same ones he wore the last time I visited, Danny thought.

"Bring it in, brother." Danny extended his arms toward Zak, who stepped forward to share a hug and a few slaps on the back.

"Dan, seriously, what's going on? I haven't heard from you in days, and now you show up at my house?"

"Can we talk about this inside?"

"Yes, of course. Apologies. Come on."

Danny followed Zak into the house, and he promptly flicked on the light switch.

His friend had put on a few pounds since they'd last seen each other, but nothing unhealthy. He otherwise appeared the same. His tousled brown hair was now streaked with gray. Thick-framed glasses rested too low on his crooked nose. And the same gentle smile made Zak one of the more likeable people in the DEA.

Danny shuffled into the living room behind his friend. "Hope I'm not disrupting anything."

"Not at all. Just finished watching the Nationals game." Zak grabbed his TV remote and turned the screen off. "Is everything okay, Dan? Can I get you a drink?"

"If you still keep beer in the fridge, I could really use one."

Zak nodded. "Let's go sit in the kitchen."

"Do you check your house and belongings for any signs of listening devices? These guys have proven they can track burner phones."

"Everyday when I get home. Check my doorbell cam and all the potential spots where something could be hidden.

"Good. Can't take any chances right now." They settled at the table while Zak opened two bottles of Corona. Danny gulped half of his down before speaking another word. "We're in trouble, Zak. You. Me. Nadia. She's heading here as we speak."

"Nadia? What kind of trouble?"

"Remember that list of names? The one you're on? It's a hit list. Steele 'hired' me to kill everyone on that list. I thought exposing Steele would be our best option, but I'm thinking we need to do something more drastic." Danny took a swig of his beer, shaking his head. "I got away with faking the death of Marcus Vance. Steele bought it—still does, I believe. But Vance sent me some documents that make for quite the case against not only Steele, but leaders in every department across D.C."

Zak gulped down his own Corona. "What documents?"

"Documents proving your boss is a sick, evil man who should probably be removed from existence." Danny opened each attachment and link on his phone and slid it across the table, content to let Zak skim through while sipping the second half of his beer. Zak's eyes widened as he scrolled, shaking his head as disappointment crawled over his face.

Zak pushed the phone back to Danny and looked up, his eyes wide. "Is this for real?"

"I can't say for sure, but Vance is retired CIA. He knows his stuff. No idea how he gathered all this, but we need to get the word out."

Zak let out a nervous laugh. "We? Dan, I'm not going to lose my job over this."

"Your job? You're working for a criminal who literally has your name on a hit list. Steele told me everyone on the list poses a risk to bringing down their illegal operation. If you're on it, I assume the rest are all good people who wouldn't be afraid to take down Steele." Danny looked his friend in the eye, allowing his words to take a pleading tone. "Zak, you're working for a madman. We need to get serious about our next steps. Exposing his corruption is a start, but we'll need to do more."

Zak took another long sip from his beer. "That may be true, but I can't get canned right now. I'm so close to cracking the security Steele put around his personal cases."

"Don't you see it, Zak? *You're* on the list. You'll lose your job one way or another. Risk getting fired or getting killed. Kill or be killed. I don't see how this is even a discussion right now. That's why I told Nadia to fly out here. The two of you can figure out how to best leak this to the press. You have the D.C. connections, and she's got the brains to devise the plan."

"Are you out of your mind, Dan?"

"*You're* not doing anything dangerous," Danny said. "All you need to do is print these files—which Nadia also has—and deliver them to the appropriate people. Make multiple copies. Spread the word as wide as you can. The more pressure we can put on Steele, the better. Hell, if you have any friends in congress, slip them a copy, too. Everything will come crashing down from there."

Zak stared at the table, running a finger up and down his beer bottle. "And what will you be doing?"

They locked eyes. “I’m going to find my mom. Then kill Charles Steele.”

CHAPTER NINETEEN

DANNY SAT in his truck outside the passenger pickup area at Dulles International.

Nadia had caught a flight that put her in D.C. at one o'clock in the morning. The airport was a ghost town. Security didn't even bother to harass those who waited too long in the pickup area.

When Nadia strolled through the sliding glass doors, Danny's stomach lurched into his throat. He scurried out of his truck and circled around to meet her.

Nadia smiled, briefcase at her side. She wore a black blazer and matching dress pants from her day at work.

Danny admired her beauty before stepping forward, his throat and thoughts both locked up.

"Hi, Danny." Nadia dropped her briefcase and opened her arms. Danny slid into her embrace and wrapped his arms around her, breathing in her familiar scent, remembering the days it used to linger on his pillows.

"Nadia. How was the flight? How are you feeling?"

Danny pulled away and grabbed her briefcase, leading her to the passenger door of his truck.

"I don't think I've ever flown somewhere so last minute. Bought my ticket one hour before the flight's departure. Rushed through security, ran down the terminals, and made it just as they were boarding the plane. Got some work done on the flight and haven't had a moment to even think about my stalker."

"You'll be safe here," Danny said. "We'll head over to Zak's place. He pulled out some clothes you can use as pajamas tonight. Obviously, everything is closed right now, but we can swing by a store first thing in the morning."

They settled into the truck, and Danny hit the road for the twenty-five-minute drive back to his friend's house.

Nadia pressed her head against the window. "It's crazy being back here, isn't it? Almost feels like our life here never stopped."

Danny turned on the truck's A/C, having noted the sweat forming around Nadia's crown. "Yeah. I've been at it ever since arriving, but it's been a walk down memory lane."

"I still think about life here in D.C. sometimes. It was one of the best periods of my life. Wouldn't trade it for anything."

Danny's stomach kept twisting into knots. They had shared their lives together in D.C. Her words were unexpected compliments, even if she didn't come out and say it directly.

He debated reaching over the center console and holding her hand. But Nadia had come out here on a leap of faith, and Danny couldn't rattle her trust in him. They'd long ago had plenty of conversations about getting back together. Would Danny move to Chicago? Or Nadia to Colorado? They never could agree, and had remained in their separate lanes.

"What do you have in store for us?" Nadia asked, running a finger along the briefcase resting on her lap.

"The main thing is to stay safe. Zak is on a hit list issued by his own boss. I'm supposed to kill him. Who knows what Steele will send our way now. Zak's not going to like it, but I'm going to propose we don't stay in his house after tonight."

Nadia rubbed her forehead. "We're not staying here? I wasn't supposed to get tied up in this mess, Danny. But they found me easily in Chicago. Already knew where I parked for work. Honestly surprised they didn't just wait for me at my house."

"They're not that obvious. For Vance, they'd already surveilled him. Knew what time he woke up in the mornings. His routine, his family's routines. What hours he'd be home alone. They were probably doing the same thing for you."

Danny didn't know if it was their return to D.C. or simply her mere presence in his truck, but everything felt right in his world. The knots in his gut vanished. His worries about surviving Steele and bringing him to justice were a minor inconvenience. Danny was with his person, whether or not they had a future together. The jelly to his peanut butter.

They continued catching up during the rest of the drive, and twenty minutes later, Danny exited the highway and worked his way into Zak's neighborhood.

Zak had promised to stay awake, and the lights in his house were all on when Danny dropped Nadia in front of the house. He parked two blocks away again and jogged back over. When he arrived, Zak and Nadia were already seated at the kitchen table, discussing Nadia's life as a district attorney in Chicago.

Fatigue clearly weighed down both Zak and Nadia. "Is there anything we need to discuss tonight?" Zak asked with an exaggerated yawn.

"You two are free to do whatever you see fit to leak these documents to the press," Danny said. "Be as discreet as you'd like. One thing I want to discuss before we call it a night is a potential hideout."

"A hideout?"

Danny sat down in the open seat between them. "I can't stay here, Zak. There are trained assassins after me. Why run the risk and endanger you? I have to go off the grid. Do you know anywhere I could stay? Doesn't have to necessarily be secluded, but somewhere no one would think to look."

Zak yawned again, balling a fist in front of his mouth. "I know a place. Hell, I may need to join you there at some point."

Zak described an abandoned cabin in the woods. He'd gone off trail during a hike once and come across it. Didn't look like anyone had been there in years. Cracked windows, door slightly off the hinges. Hell, it's possible a bear had tried to get in at some point. But after checking it out through the windows, he'd gone inside. Everything was covered in dust, and the kitchen looked like it fell out of the Eighties. But it had a bed, a couch, and an outhouse around the back.

"I take it you've gone back?" Danny asked.

Zak nodded. "Tried looking up the property in our systems at the DEA, but nothing comes up for it. Must have been built without permits. I've gone back a handful of times just to see if anyone ever showed up. Never saw any sign of another person."

"How far from here?"

"About forty minutes. I can write down the exact directions for getting there. It's about a mile off the trail, maybe a little less."

Danny shook his head. "Aren't people supposed to *not* go off trail? Especially when they're alone?"

Zak shrugged. "It's the curiosity. The founders of this country roamed those same woods with no technology. That reminds me, you will pass a series of unmarked graves—I'm guessing they're from the Civil War. Once you see those, you're more than halfway there."

Danny's phone buzzed, and he fumbled the old burner out of his pocket.

"Someone's messaging you right now?" Nadia asked. "It's almost two in the morning. Christ, I need to go to bed."

Danny placed the phone on the table and glared at it. "It's Steele."

He opened the message to find no text, but an attached video. It was slightly distorted by choppy pixelation, but he recognized his mother.

The video played, showing Steele enter his mother's room.

"Who's there?" she called out.

"Hi, Ms. Cortez." Steele approached her in her wheelchair and dropped to a knee. He took her hands in his.

Don't touch my mother, you low life.

"Who are you?!" his mom shouted.

She didn't sound like herself, and a pang of guilt shot into Danny's chest.

"Ms. Cortez," Steele continued. "I'm a close friend of your son, Danny. Do you remember him?"

"Of course I know my own son. What do you want?"

"I'm sorry to say that Danny was murdered while working on a secret mission. I thought you should know. Please tell us if you need anything."

Without another word, Steele released Tatiana's hands and left the room. But the video kept rolling.

Tatiana whimpered and buried her face in her hands. She cried, "Why, God? Take me instead. I have nothing left!"

She rolled over to her nightstand, grabbed the lamp, and threw it against the wall. "Why God? Not my Danny."

Danny's entire body tensed as he watched the video, which ended after showing his mother crying for another fifteen seconds. He dialed Steele, fuming.

Steele answered while Nadia and Zak watched Danny with wide eyes. "Danny! I didn't expect you to call me at this hour."

Danny all but growled into the phone. "What have you done to my mother?"

"Me?" Steele asked with mock offense. "What have *you* done, Danny? Weren't thinking about your mother when you took those illegal documents for a joy ride, were you? I'm calling the shots here. And I'm willing to give you one more chance, assuming you haven't shared those documents with anyone else."

"Why does that matter? They're not even mine. The person who sent them could already be sharing them."

"We're working on that. I'm not concerned. I've done some reflecting. You simply received those files. That doesn't mean you're colluding against me." Steele paused and took what sounded like a drink of water. "What I did to your mother was emotional damage. Psychological. She thinks her only son is dead and will slowly believe she'll never escape. If you don't do as I say, the next step in our plans will be physical harm." His snicker filled Danny with cold rage. "I'd really hate to do that to such a sweet old lady."

"I could share these files right now," Danny said. "Forward them to every press in the country."

"And if you do that, you'll receive your mother's head in a box. So let's not make bad choices."

"What do you want from me?"

"I only want what you owe me, Danny. You've already removed Marcus Vance from this world. Now, kill Eva Ramirez."

CHAPTER TWENTY

DANNY HAD STRUGGLED to sleep overnight. Both because of the mounting pressure from Steele—Danny couldn't erase the visual of his weeping mother from his mind—and knowing Nadia slept in the guest room next to his. His current predicament was a cocktail of emotions he lacked the energy to deal with.

One thing at a time.

Danny received a text message from Niko the next morning.

It included the home address and an estimated daily schedule for Eva Ramirez. Niko included a side note mentioning Eva was currently unemployed and her daily routines could change without notice.

He projected her to remain in her house most of the week, citing the only time she left was to either run to the grocery store or stop at the gym three days a week, the timing of which varied.

Niko had dug into Eva's digital footprint as well, finding she had not yet applied to any other jobs.

Enjoying the time off? Danny wondered.

He expected Eva would not take kindly to a request to fake her death. Having just lost a job, her emotions could be all over the place.

Nadia would likely sleep in late, and Danny had no time to waste. He left a note for both her and Zak explaining where he would be and stated his plans to stay at Zak's hideout for the remainder of his time in the D.C. area.

He ended with a plea for Zak to let Nadia borrow his car for a quick run to the store.

Both of them snored while Danny rummaged through the kitchen for breakfast. When the clock struck eight, he slipped out the front door with a banana and a granola bar and jogged to his truck two blocks away.

The humidity clung to his skin, even at the early hour. When he got out of this mess—if he got out—he decided he'd move somewhere without this suffocating dampness.

Danny started his truck and plugged Eva's address into the GPS. She lived a couple of towns south in Newington, about twenty minutes away. Better yet, it lay on the route toward the hideout.

Being Saturday morning, Danny had the roads to himself. He blasted down the freeway, arriving in Eva's neighborhood in only fifteen minutes. She lived on a crowded block, which would complicate matters if she made a scene out of Danny's appearance at her front door. An older couple at the end of the block sat on their front porch, drinking from mugs of coffee and watching the birds enjoy their breakfast from the feeder standing on the lawn.

Two houses down from them, a man mowed his lawn, headphones snug over his ears as sweat trickled down his shirtless body.

Danny drove past and stopped directly in front of Eva's house, scanning the area for any signs of surveillance.

Spotting nothing suspicious, he jumped out of his truck and marched up to Eva's front door. She kept an assortment of plants and flowers on the porch. The welcome mat at his feet had sunflower decorations around the perimeter.

Danny knocked and took a step back. The door lacked a peephole, so he glanced at the nearby windows, looking for movement inside. He saw nothing, but a few seconds later, the door opened a crack, and Danny found himself staring down the black holes of a double-barreled shotgun.

He raised his hands.

"Who are you?" a voice called out. Someone toed the door open another few inches, revealing Eva Ramirez, her brown eyes locked onto Danny's.

Danny cleared his throat. "Hello, Ms. Ramirez. My name is Danny Cortez. I'm an ex-DEA intelligence analyst. Charles Steele has hired me against my will to kill you. I have no intention of doing that and would like to discuss how we can both get out of this situation alive."

"Steele," she muttered, not hiding the disgust in her voice.

"He's holding my mother hostage until I complete his hit list," Danny said, keeping his voice steady and neutral. "The first name on my list was Marcus Vance, a retired DEA agent. We faked his death, and he's currently hiding until this scandal is resolved."

"Who is *we*?" she demanded.

"I have a friend in the Chicago D.A. office. She is a master of fake obituaries and other pertinent death documents."

Silence sat between them. Eva would have pulled that trigger already if she believed Danny posed a threat.

Instead, she lowered the shotgun, keeping it gripped in both hands. "What do you know?"

"I know a lot, Ms. Ramirez. And I can assure you I'm on your side."

"How can *I* know that?"

"If I wanted to kill you, Ms. Ramirez, I wouldn't have knocked on your front door."

He had used this same line on Vance, and it appeared to have the same effect this time around. She released one hand from the shotgun and held it to her side. "Come in. I still want to pat you down. And call me Eva. Ms. Ramirez sounds like my grandma."

Eva stepped back and allowed Danny to enter her home. She laid her shotgun against the wall and pulled a revolver out of the table drawer next to the door.

"Just being safe." Keeping the revolver trained on his back, she dropped to one knee and frisked him; legs, waist, and torso.

When she finished, she stood up and slipped the revolver back into the drawer. Danny had his first actual glimpse of the woman.

Eva stood as tall as he did. She had a thick, muscular build that resembled a professional MMA fighter. She wore a black tank top, showing off several arm tattoos. By Danny's estimate, she had at least twenty pounds over him. All pure muscle.

"Tell me everything you know," she demanded. "And I'll know if you're lying, so don't even think about it."

Danny rarely experienced intimidation, and Eva was bringing the heat. "They've been watching you, Eva. I don't know *who* exactly, but I received a message with your address and routine. Ever since you got fired, you've only left the house for the gym and grocery store."

"I knew it." Eva clapped her hands together, then balled them into fists. "These dummies think I'm new to the game, but I was with the CIA for seven years. I can recognize an unfamiliar car parked on my block for several days at a time." She scoffed. "My gym is in the guest room, but once I thought I was being watched, I started driving to the gym in town to see if they'd follow me. They followed me alright but never went inside. Such cowards."

"I'm sorry, Ms. Ram—Eva—but why did you even think someone was following you?"

"They might tell you I was fired for insubordination, but that's just a cover. The insubordination, if you can call it that, was me asking why a particular case was transferred from me to another agent. That's it. A simple question. Didn't even have a tone when I asked. But they fired me on the spot."

"I take it you were actually close to busting them and their entire scheme of dominating the international drug ring." Danny recognized her tone. It was the case that got away from Eva. The type that would keep her up many nights, dwelling on where things had gone wrong.

Eva clenched her jaw. "I sure was. How did you end up involved with this?"

"I helped capture Victor Villa the first time and did it solo the second time after his escape."

"That was *you*?"

"Don't sound so shocked." Danny laughed. Eva was probably making the same judgments of him based off his physical appearance.

Eva looked him up and down. "I don't take you as a field agent. Scrawny little guy. I could throw you through a wall."

Danny chuckled. "I don't doubt that. But apparently, Steele saw my talent as beneficial to his cause. I wouldn't say he trusts me. It's more he trusts his blackmail over me."

"Your mom."

"Exactly." It was refreshing speaking with someone who could follow along with the several moving parts of this robust scheme.

"What a sick man." Eva shook her head, face scrunched like she had just smelled a rotten egg. "I know plenty. I'd been doing lots of research on my own. I haven't been able to find who everything is tied to, though."

"Did you tell anyone about your suspicions?"

"Hell no! I wanted to, but once I discovered people within the CIA were involved, I kept all my notes to myself. If I don't know who to trust, I won't say a damn thing."

"Well, I trust you, Eva. And I know for a fact Senator Calloway's calling the shots."

"He was on my short list. I just couldn't make the connection to prove it." Eva smirked and crossed her arms across her bosom. "How do you know for sure?"

"My first target was Marcus Vance. He sent me the notes he'd been compiling on his own."

"Vance?" Eva asked, her eyes lighting with recognition. "Thought I recognized the name when you first said it. I know him. He's been retired. Wait, Vance is who agreed to let you fake his death?"

Danny nodded, rubbing the back of his neck. "Not just him, but his wife and kids. They're all in on it. Apparently, he'd seen enough to understand his life was in danger and wanted to go along."

"Damn. I wish I had known I could've trusted him. I'd actually considered reaching out to him about it but didn't want to bother him since he's retired."

"How did you know him?" Danny asked. "I don't recall him ever being with the CIA."

"He wasn't. But we worked with him on locating drug cartels in North America. He'd tell us about the ones with operations in the States, and we'd find their bases in other countries. I always thought he was one of the more competent people in the DEA. No offense."

"None taken. So, what do you think? Are you open to faking your death to get these goons off our trail?"

CHAPTER TWENTY-ONE

THEY MOVED into the living room, Eva taking a seat on the couch while Danny settled on the cushioned chair on the opposite side.

"I'm not faking my death." Eva crossed her arms, daring Danny to continue his fight. "That's a coward's move, and I'm no coward."

Danny traced the lined patterns on the chair's armrest with his finger. "You can't think of it as a coward's move, Eva. These people are dangerous. If I don't make it seem like I killed you, they'll just do it themselves."

Eva laughed, but her face remained a stone. "You want to write an obituary and send me into hiding? I'm so close. I have many things in the works that are secured should I end up dead. But I'm not going to die. Real or fake."

Eva crossed her legs and glared across the room.

"I'm clearly not going to win this argument, am I?"

Eva shook her head.

"Fine. Then we'll adjust our plans."

"I'm willing to face this head on," she said. "Are you?"

"That's easy for you to say," he replied. "You only have to worry about yourself. I'm being threatened to kill multiple people or risk losing my mother. I'm trying to play this is as fairly to everyone as I can. All without losing any lives."

"Haven't you thought about how this ends?" Eva asked, narrowing her eyes.

"In what sense?"

"What makes you think they'll let you live even if you complete their hit list? These are cruel, disgusting people. They know how to make people disappear, dead or alive. If I may be blunt, your compliance is your biggest mistake. You won't magically become a non-threat to their operation. You finish the list, they give your mother back, and the next day they put a bullet between your eyes and toss you over a bridge."

Danny chuckled, masking his nerves. He had considered this before, but had yet to hear it put so bluntly. "That may be so, but I'm working with what I have. My disobedience will guarantee my mother's torture and death. And they'll make sure I see it."

Eva tilted her head back and brushed her chin. "If it were up to me, I'd have gotten all the people on the list together to make a plan. If they're on the list, they know something. Having all those minds in the same room would generate some ideas for how to take them down."

Danny hadn't considered that. "Would also put a major target on our backs," he said. "If they saw all their targets gathered in the same place, wouldn't they arrange an attack to wipe us all out? They wouldn't even care about collateral damage at that point. As long as their threats were all eliminated."

Eva tossed her hands up. "I'm just saying there are other options. It's great Vance is actually alive, and that Steele believes otherwise. Your friend must be fantastic at her job."

Danny's phone vibrated in his pocket and he stood to fish it out. An inbound phone call. He frowned at it.

"Something wrong?" Eva asked.

He raised a finger and answered the phone. "Zak?"

Zak wasted no time, delivering his message with urgency. Danny could only nod, even though his friend couldn't see him. After ten seconds, he nervously glanced around for the windows. His sudden movement made Eva rise from her seat, too.

He hung up and stuffed the phone back in his pocket. "We have to leave. Right now."

"Leave? Why?"

"We've been spotted. Friend of mine in the DEA said he caught word they're sending a group after us. They're on the way right now."

"I'll drive." Eva dashed to her key table next to the front door and scooped up her phone, jamming it into her pocket.

"No. Let's take my truck."

"Where are we going?" Eva's voice remained calm and focused.

"I have a place."

Danny was already speeding around the table to get to the front door. Eva opened her mouth to speak but stopped when tires screeched to a halt outside. She glanced at the drawer near her front door.

"They're here," Danny cried. "We have to slip through the back now."

He wasn't leaving without her. They glanced out the window. Four men charged toward the house, guns in hand.

Eva dashed to her entryway and grabbed her revolver out of the drawer. She handed it to Danny and picked up her shotgun from the wall. "Out the back door and go left. There's a gate that's half open."

Danny nodded. "Run like hell to my truck. I'll cover you."

"We cover each other. Let's go."

They turned and darted toward the back of the house. Eva yanked the door open and closed it gently after them just as a thunderous bang came from inside. The front door being kicked open.

"Go!" Eva whispered, pushing Danny toward the side of the house.

She ran around him to take the lead and turned the corner. They had to step over and through piles of rocks, bricks, and plant pots. They reached the gate, and Eva slipped through its opening, Danny's truck only thirty feet away.

She glanced over her shoulder, and he pointed his chin toward the truck, eyes wide.

Eva broke into a sprint for the truck, Danny trailing on her hip. When they were within fifteen feet, a man on her porch shouted. "They went out the back! They're running!" A second man stepped out of the front door and opened fire.

Gunfire erupted behind them. Danny blasted several shots in the men's direction, seeing at least one of them collapse to the ground. Two rounds planted into the truck's passenger door just as they reached the vehicle. Eva fumbled with the door's handle, opened it and leaped inside. Four more rounds were fired at them.

Danny's eyes swam with a laser focus as he hurried around his truck and jumped into the driver's seat. Two men lay dead on Eva's front porch, one sprawled on top of the other blood oozing from their chests. Their guns lay limp in their nonexistent grip. In a swift motion, he stuck the key in the ignition and put the truck into gear.

Danny accelerated forward and forced his wheel to the right, turning the truck around and leaving dark tire marks on the pavement. As they circled back, two more men appeared in Eva's front door. One raced for his SUV while the other held his pistol in both hands, lining up a shot.

The man fired. Danny rolled down his window, right hand on the steering wheel, left sticking out with the revolver. He shot back. The man dove out of the way. One round left. Danny lowered the revolver to the SUV's front tire and shot. It deflated on the spot.

Danny sped out of the neighborhood. In the rearview mirror, he spotted the second man examining the busted tire. The guy punched the side of the SUV and stomped his feet like an enraged child.

Danny panted for breath, wiping the sweat off his brow with his forearm. "They won't be following us."

"Who the hell was that?" Eva kept checking the mirrors for the next five blocks until they were convinced no one had followed them. "Who called to tell you they were coming?"

"You might know him. Zak Larocque."

She was silent for a moment, panting as another familiar name seemed to dawn on her. "Larocque from the DEA?"

Danny nodded. "He's one of my best friends. He's been trying to hack Steele's agency accounts to read his emails and private messages." He swallowed, taking a moment to catch his breath. "He hacked in and saw a note this morning about killing both of us at your house. We got lucky, Eva. We should be dead."

CHAPTER TWENTY-TWO

FINDING ZAK'S hideout almost pushed Danny to the brink of insanity.

When his friend had first given him the directions, Danny only checked the initial few steps, which included where to drive and turn off the road. This got them to the correct area.

From there, the directions became vaguer.

Walk 30 steps and turn left.

At the tree with a heart carved into it, continue 45 degrees to the northeast.

Five other steps followed with similar clarity. But then Danny found the unmarked gravestones Zak had mentioned, reassuring him he was on the right track.

Eva trailed behind him, sweating but never complaining. The mosquitoes preferred Eva's blood to Danny's. She smacked her skin every two minutes as they trudged through the heavily wooded forest.

"Are you sure this place really exists?" she asked after Danny stopped and examined the area. Trees surrounded them in every direction, providing a sense they were alone in the world. Perhaps on an entirely different planet.

"Zak wouldn't make all this up."

After surviving the attack at Eva's house and hiking through the woods for the past twenty minutes, Danny had grown irritable and hungry. The banana and granola bar from earlier had only been meant to hold him until lunch.

"It should be forty more steps." Danny continued forward, his worry growing with each passing second. They had no compass and had left no breadcrumbs to follow back to the truck. They pushed through the stand of trees.

Eva laughed. "Forty steps. We should be able to see it then."

Danny agreed, and after only thirty, the trees separated into a clearing that encircled the cabin.

Relief flooded Danny like he'd just found a well of water after roaming the desert for a week.

Eva shuffled up next to him and they studied the cabin. The cracked windows made it difficult to see inside, but the door hung slightly ajar on its rusted hinges.

"Hello?" Danny called out. He turned to Eva and shrugged. "Just in case."

She laughed again. "Right. Because so many people have stumbled across this random cabin that I'm pretty sure is haunted. Let's go in and see what we're dealing with."

Eva pushed past Danny and marched up to the door, struggling to pull it open as the hinges whined and groaned. A squirrel darted out of the cabin and vanished up a tree.

"Not exactly at the top of my Airbnb wish list," she said.

Danny strolled up behind and followed her into the cabin.

Cobwebs decorated the corners and ceiling. A crooked wooden table stood in the kitchen, pots and pans scattered on its surface. A coal-powered oven waited in the corner, assuming it still worked. The sofa in the living room in front of them had gashes with cotton sticking out. A stack of blankets towered on the floor, covered in dust.

"Just needs a good cleaning," Danny said. "We have sturdy walls and a roof. Don't need much else right now."

"With no cleaning supplies?" Eva looked around the decrepit room. "I don't even see a broom anywhere."

"I'll head back into town and get supplies," Danny said. "No saying how long we'll be staying here."

"You really want to hide here? I want to fight these guys, Danny. They broke into my house."

Someone has to keep their cool and think logically.

"I'm all for eliminating these people—they're the ones who actually deserve it. But there is so much up in the air right now. We were spotted and attacked at your house. Does Steele know? I assume so. And does that mean he's changed his beliefs about me? Did they see it as us colluding together? If so, he could have doubts about Vance now. If Steele has completely lost trust in me, which I believe he has, then he won't stop until I'm dead.

"I don't see this cabin as a place to hide until everything blows over. I see it as a refuge where I can think in peace and not worry about looking over my shoulder every two seconds. You saw how hard this place was to find. Even if they find my truck parked at the trailhead, they have no way of accidentally coming across us."

"I'm not denying this place is safe," Eva said, crossing her arms. "It's clearly way off the grid." She was silent for a moment, chewing the inside of her cheek. "A refuge is a good idea. We can make plans here, go back into society, raise hell, and return here. It's a lot of work, but worth it."

"Glad we're on the same page." Danny pulled out his cell phone. "I don't have any signal out here. Do you?"

Eva checked. "I do. One bar, but it's there."

"Keep it off until we need to communicate with Zak to find out what's going on. I'm gonna head into town and get supplies. And food. Do you wanna hang out here and spruce things up?"

She scoffed. "I'll do what I can."

"Message me if you think of anything else we need from the store. My main priorities are cleaning supplies, food, and water. Don't forget to turn off the phone if you use it."

Eva nodded. "Toilet paper!"

CHAPTER TWENTY-THREE

AFTER HIS TRIP INTO TOWN, Danny returned to a tidied cabin. Eva had shaken the mattress and bed sheets free of the dust that'd plagued them. She separated the stack of blankets across the living room sofa to form a makeshift bed for herself.

Equipped with a broom, mop, and disinfectant wipes, the two of them spent three hours cleaning the cabin. Their hands appeared charred with muck by the end, and they ventured to a nearby creek to wash off the grime.

After cleaning, they sat at the kitchen table and enjoyed a dinner of chicken tenders and mashed potatoes Danny had picked up from the grocery. Though at room temperature by the time they ate, the flavor and portions satisfied their appetites.

Danny had stocked up on non-perishable foods and stacked the cans of fruits and veggies next to the old oven. Boxes of crackers and other snacks filled the lone cabinet. He'd also bought new hinges and replaced them on the door. The only defect remaining was the cracked window, which Eva had hung a blanket over as a drape.

Danny headed to bed after dinner, desperate for sleep after being up late the night before. Eva had said she would stay up another couple of hours before calling it a night.

Danny had slept for almost six hours when he woke up in his pitch-black room. It was 1:14 in the morning. He remained there, tossing and turning. The day had left him exhausted, and his frustration boiled over when he didn't drift back off. As much as he willed himself back to sleep, his mind and body refused to cooperate.

The ground crunched outside. Animals moving around in the night. He had spotted plenty of deer and opossums during his venture back and forth from his truck. The forest also served as home to black bears, raccoons, foxes, and bobcats. Nothing he wished to confront in the middle of the night.

His mother pressed on his thoughts. Had Steele already tortured her? Danny doubted Steele would do anything unless he could show the proof. He could have recorded such a travesty and sent another video, but Danny's phone still had no signal at the cabin. No way of knowing if Steele had reached out to taunt him.

After an hour of rolling around to find the perfect position, Danny drifted off to sleep.

When he awoke next, a bright glow flickered from the living room.

Danny didn't know how long he'd been asleep, but his brain remained clouded with exhaustion. He rolled out of bed, stumbling in the dark toward the living room. The bedroom had no door, so he passed through the frame by feeling around with extended hands.

"Eva?" Danny called out, sure the glow had also woken her. Or she was the source. "Eva, what—"

Danny stepped into the living room and froze.

Flames flickered along the cabin's only door. Danny coughed, smoke filling his lungs. He dropped low and shouted. "Eva!"

Eva mumbled something from the couch, her body rolling off with a thud moments later.

The flames spread rapidly, swallowing the door and extending to the adjoined walls. The fire cast enough of a glow for Danny to see into the kitchen. He dashed across the room and pulled out two water bottles.

Eva jumped up just as Danny unscrewed the lids from the bottles.

"What the hell?" she shouted, her voice wide awake.

Danny approached the flames and squeezed the bottle, spraying water across the door. It went out in patches but continued spreading across the walls.

"Stay calm," Danny said, completely panicking on the inside.

"How do we get out?" Eva replied. She ran to the window in the kitchen and yanked the blanket off. She jumped back and shrieked at the sight of tall flames waving from the outside. "The cabin's on fire, Danny! The whole thing!"

In the thirty seconds they'd been in the living room, the flames had extended into every wall. The smoke inside thickened, and they both dropped to the floor. The crackling grew louder as the temperature climbed.

I'm going to burn to death in this cabin, and no one will ever know. Not until Zak finds me months later.

Flames covered the interior, now spreading to the ceiling above. The cabin had no fire-proofing and would burn no differently from a bonfire in the middle of the mountains. Spotting the smoke in the middle of the night would be impossible for anyone to see from a distance.

"Throw me a blanket," Danny shouted across the room. He had dropped to the floor near the kitchen, while Eva had crawled toward the living room sofa. It became bright inside, like floodlights had been switched on.

They regarded each other through the black smoke filling the room.

Eva hacked into her hands before snatching a blanket off the sofa and tossing it toward Danny. He drew in a deep breath, wrapped himself in the blanket, and stood up. He planned to march toward the door and attempt opening it with the blanket as protection from the surely burning doorknob.

Before he could reach the door, a crack sounded from above. The roof caved in and completely collapsed. Logs of wood and chunks of debris fell straight onto the sofa. And onto Eva.

"No!" Danny shouted.

Eva shrieked. A burning log had fallen directly on her back, pinning her to the floor. She writhed and twisted her body trying to break free, but her face-down position and the weight of the log made it impossible.

"Help, Danny!" she screamed, fear and desperation dominating her voice. "It burns!"

Danny tossed the blanket aside and lunged toward the log. It had to weigh at least five hundred pounds. Assisted by adrenaline, Danny squatted and used the power in his legs to pull the log. He gritted his teeth, screaming and grunting while every muscle fiber in his body concentrated its effort on the log.

He raised it just enough for Eva to wriggle out from under it. She crawled away from the sofa, using only her arms, while Danny dropped the log.

He drew in a deep breath of smoke, which triggered a nasty coughing attack. "C'mon!"

Danny reached down for Eva's hands and pulled her up.

"I can't move my legs!" she cried.

Eva collapsed onto Danny, her dead weight shoving him off balance. She, too, swallowed a gulp of smoke and broke into an uncontrollable coughing fit.

The smoke dissipated through the collapsed roof, providing a moment of relief. Yet, the fire surrounded them at every turn. They needed to escape the cabin or die.

Danny slung his arm around Eva's waist, pulling her tightly against his hip. "Hold on to me as best you can."

Her eyes fluttered, rolling back and forth as she fought off unconsciousness. She mumbled incoherently.

Danny pulled Eva toward the couch, which had just caught its first flames, and grabbed another blanket resting over its edge. "Let's go."

He wrapped the blanket over both of them and clambered toward the flame-engulfed door. Heat radiated from the surface, searing Danny's face as if he had just opened an oven.

Danny had no time to spare. Balling a portion of the blanket around his hand, he grabbed the rusty doorknob. The scorching heat still seeped through the blanket, but in one quick second on the knob, he jerked the door open.

Danny dragged Eva through the doorway, giant flames flickering above their heads and below their feet. He jumped over the fire and yanked Eva along. The blanket caught fire, so Danny let it slip behind them.

"Almost there," he grunted, pulling Eva through the dirt and away from the cabin.

Once they were at least one hundred feet away, Danny lowered Eva to the ground, her head bobbing from side to side, and rested her back against a tree trunk.

Danny fell next to her, panting for breath, lungs screaming in protest. "We made it."

For the next several hours, he watched the cabin burn to a mere pile of ash, knowing exactly who had set it ablaze.

And wondering how they had found their hideout.

CHAPTER TWENTY-FOUR

DANNY STAYED at Eva's side until she woke three hours later.

The sun cracked over the horizon, revealing a smoking pile of rubble with smaller flames still clinging to their lives.

The two had used the tree trunk as their bed for the long night outside. Danny couldn't sleep while the cabin burned. When the raging flames dwindled, however, he nodded off, his shoulder pressed against Eva's.

The mosquitoes that had plagued them throughout the day fled the smoke and never returned. Any wildlife they might have worried about would take no chances approaching the smoldering building.

Combined with the sleep Danny had before the fire, he counted nearly eight hours in total. Yet, fatigue weighed on him.

When Eva stirred, Danny jumped to his feet to pivot and face her straight on. Her head bobbed around, eyes fluttering while guttural noises escaped her throat.

"What happened?" she asked through dry, cracked lips.

Her eyes opened all the way, searching Danny's face for answers, then looking past him to see what had become of the cabin they just spent all afternoon cleaning.

"They found us," Danny said. He dropped to one knee for a more direct view. "I have no idea how. But they seemed to think burning the cabin should have taken care of us. No one has been around all night to check on the status of their arson."

"How do you know it was them?"

"Who else would do that? Never mind the long odds of them finding our hideout. But just think of who would set the cabin ablaze, knowing we were inside."

"Could have been natural."

Danny shook his head, balling a fist. "No, Eva. You're clearly not thinking straight. There is no electricity here. No gas lines. Not even the coal oven had any coal inside of it. There weren't other people in the woods messing around with campfires." He looked directly into her eyes, hoping to get through. "This was a targeted attack meant to kill us in our sleep. That cabin might've been two hundred years old. They *knew* it would burn fast."

Eva dropped her head and rubbed her legs where the log had fallen. Danny had examined her while she slept and found nothing but intense bruising along her legs. Nothing appeared broken, but only a trained doctor could tell for sure.

"Think you can walk back to the truck?" he asked her.

Eva leaned her head back against the tree, two small tears streaming down her face. "I don't know, Danny. I can't feel my legs right now. Guessing that's not a good sign."

"You're gonna have to try," he said. "We've got to get out of here. Bounce around different hotels until we figure out our next steps."

Eva nodded and stretched out a mud-covered hand. "Help me up."

Danny stood and grabbed Eva's hand, pulling her to her feet.

She winced and sucked in air through her teeth, promptly leaning against the tree. "It hurts, alright. Dammit."

"I didn't see any breaks. What do you think?"

Eva shook her head. "I don't think anything's broken. Some of the feeling is coming back, but if I put weight on either leg, pain shoots all the way up my back."

"What do you want to do?"

Eva studied the cabin's remnants, then the woods. "We've gotta walk back. It's going to take a while, and I'll need several breaks. But I can push through. There's too much we need to do, and this is a golden opportunity."

"Golden opportunity?" Danny asked. "You can't even walk."

Eva glared at him, her feistiness returning to her eyes. "I'm dead, Danny. As far as any of those people with their hit list are concerned, I'm dead. Do you understand?"

"I can be dead, too."

Excitement blossomed within Danny. This truly was a unique chance to take a fresh approach. How could they ever anticipate Danny's next move if they believed him dead?

Eva shook her head, bringing Danny back to earth. "No. You're still alive. We have to get to your truck and leave. They'll know your truck is gone and that you're alive. Even if they're not tracking your truck, you should still be up front with them, especially Steele. Make up a story. Tell him you were scared to kill me and made this plan to lure me into the woods where you could do it in privacy. Say you were going to kill me in the morning, but the fire took care of it. You escaped. Hide me wherever. I'm gonna need a few days to get back on my feet, anyway. But I have an idea."

He waited for her to share it. When she didn't, he asked, "What is it?"

"I'm not sharing it yet. Could be crazy. Need to think through it first."

Danny gritted his teeth but understood. He looked at the path ahead of them, not even bothering to turn back to the cabin and grab their belongings that had surely turned to ash.

"Let's get started then."

"All the water's gone, isn't it?"

Danny nodded. "Water. Snacks. Nothing left. There is a second case of water in the truck, though. Couldn't carry two with all the other bags wrapped around my arms."

"That's fine," she said. "It'll motivate me to keep walking. Let's go."

Eva pushed off the tree, and Danny wrapped his arm around her waist. Together, they started away from the cabin. Having already made a round trip, Danny was comfortable with the route back to the hiking trail.

The morning was warm, but still manageable. The brutal heat would come after noon.

On their first break, after five hundred feet, Danny checked his phone for the time, finding it was 7:47.

Birds tweeted from high in the trees as a slight breeze tickled the leaves. In any other circumstance, he would've considered it a beautiful walk through the woods. Eva powered through every assisted step. Wincing. Groaning. Cursing to the heavens about the pain spreading across her body.

At one point, she fell silent during their walk, but tears poured from her face, splashing on her clothes. On the ground.

Danny did his best to carry the brunt of her weight. He'd considered carrying her on his back for stretches at a time, but his lower back struggled with aches of its own. Probably from lifting that damned log. At least his ankle held up after the extensive rehab in Arizona.

The conversation lagged. All of Eva's concentration focused on her pain instead of small talk. They were both hungry and dehydrated. Nothing was worth a discussion until Eva spoke about halfway through their journey back to the truck.

"I've been thinking about what you said. About Senator Calloway."

Danny kept his gaze trained forward. "What about him?"

"His involvement was the final piece for me. Everything makes sense now."

"The final piece of what?"

"For the past year, the CIA has been working on projects in South America. On the surface, the projects are all about ridding corruption and cartel influence from certain countries. Colombia. Venezuela. Argentina. Peru, you know the list. I was involved in the early stages of these projects. Identify potential threats within these governments or cartels. Assess what we can actually do. Mind you, we have to identify threats relevant to the U.S. to take any action."

"Of course."

"So that's what I did. With the help of your buddy Steele, a team of agents and I worked on connecting the dots between several known drug and arms dealers in the U.S. back to their cartels in foreign countries. That gave the CIA free rein to do as they pleased regarding those involved. But when that work was completed, most of us were released from the project and given other assignments."

"Sounds like what happened in the DEA."

"And I didn't know that," she said, glancing at Danny. "I had concerns and voiced them to my superiors. They assured me I'd done a fantastic job and that my services were simply needed elsewhere. Claimed they were deprioritizing the South America cases to spread resources to other assignments. I accepted that and moved on with my life."

"They lied, huh?"

Eva blinked rapidly. "Huge liars. I ran into a colleague outside of work, one I'd worked with on those initial projects. He told me how stressed they were from the extra hours. How they kept cutting the staff involved with those cases until it was just a dozen agents remaining. Mind you, an assignment like this would require something north of fifty agents. He then complained about how those of us who were removed had easy assignments. And it was true. Our work became trivial all of a sudden. You'd think terrorism had ceased to exist in the world based on our workload. And that's when I started digging.

"To make a long story short, the CIA's main goal with this project is to destabilize the governments in these countries. And not for some patriotic reason like killing the drug cartels. It's to control those cartels. It's a silent coup against those countries, and the CIA removed anyone who questioned the intent of the projects and following assignments. Loyalty over anything else is all they demanded. And guess who introduced the legislation that sparked all of this?"

"Senator Calloway?"

"Senator freaking Calloway."

Danny grinned. "What a slimeball. Just like most politicians, I suppose."

"That's where my investigations ended," Eva said. "But I found enough to take Calloway down. Just need the right approach."

"What if the accusations come from those countries directly?"

"What do you mean?" Eva frowned.

"It's obvious Calloway has his fingers in every department. I also wouldn't be surprised if he's corrupted members of the press. It's too risky trusting anyone in the D.C. area right now. Hell, most of the country for that matter. If these stories originate from a different country—where Calloway has been running his illegal operations—we can trust the story will break and Calloway won't know in advance."

"And how the hell would we do that?"

Danny smiled. "I've made some friends. My counterparts in some of those countries. Let me reach out and see what they can do."

CHAPTER TWENTY-FIVE

WHEN THEY REACHED the clearing near the main trail's parking lot, Eva insisted Danny check the area for any wandering eyes.

Because of the beautiful morning weather, nearly three dozen vehicles were crammed into the lot. A handful of people had just arrived, stretching and drinking water to prepare for their hike.

Danny wandered around the lot as if he couldn't find his truck, secretly checking inside the other parked vehicles. He found no one inside of them and glanced around at the surrounding trees. If anyone had eyes on him, it was from a distance out of his range.

He eventually approached his truck and dropped to both knees to check underneath. Having survived a car bomb in the past, Danny no longer took chances when he left his truck unattended for longer than an hour.

No bomb.

Surprised the truck is even still here.

If the arsonist goons had found the cabin, they certainly wouldn't have missed his truck in the lot.

Danny returned to the woods where Eva remained and helped her hobble to his truck. All the bystanders had begun their hikes, so the parking lot remained empty for them.

"Drive south," she said, once they hit the road.

He glanced in his rearview mirror. "Why?"

"If they're expecting you, they'll think you're heading north. Back toward my house. Back to D.C." Eva winced as she shifted in her seat. "They won't have a reason to believe you'll head south, because that would mean you're giving up. Which, for some reason, you refuse to do."

"Would you run away if someone kidnapped your mom?"

"No, of course not. But I'd have taken a different approach. That's all."

Danny lacked the energy to argue. And so did Eva.

They drove in silence until reaching the college town of Fredericksburg. They found two motels directly off the freeway. Danny pulled into one of their parking lots. He turned off the engine as Eva said, "I have a confession."

Danny stared at her, waiting for her to continue. When she didn't, he said, "Yes?"

"The fire is my fault. I just know it. They probably tracked my cell phone."

"Didn't you have the GPS turned off?"

"That doesn't matter. If the CIA was involved, they can track down a phone based on the last signal it received. They could've tapped into satellites that spotted us walking to the cabin. The technology can pinpoint anyone in the world, unless they're off the grid."

Danny chuckled. "I've been giving it some thought, going off the grid. Getting rid of all the technology I own. If my life stays this dangerous, I won't really have a choice."

"I'm sorry, Danny. I wasn't thinking straight. Being chased out of my own house left a mark on me. And then getting a fire started on me when I thought I was safe. I've seen some stuff in my line of work, but that was just…horrific."

Danny nodded. "You have nothing to apologize for. If anything, the fire proves how desperate they are. That wasn't a simple journey, even if you know exactly where to go. If they went through all that trouble to kill us, then we're on to something."

"I know. We just have to get the word out. And that's exactly what I plan on figuring out while I'm immobile these next few days. All while staying under wraps. No digital trail."

"You're sure you don't want a ride to the hospital?"

Eva jerked her head from side to side. "No time. That will only complicate things. Have my name appear in records. Assuming no one saw us driving, we've got to let them believe I'm dead." Eva pointed at Danny. "Call Steele and tell him what happened. Sound scared, like you had no idea something so terrifying could happen, but also like you're determined to finish the hit list. They'll like that."

"And you're going to hang out at this motel?" Danny asked. "When should I expect to see or hear from you?"

Eva grinned. "Don't worry about me, Danny. I appreciate the concern, but I can handle myself. My phone is off, and I won't turn it back on unless there is an absolute emergency. You'll hear from me in some form. Keep an eye on the news. I'll be making a move, and I'm sure it'll cause some ripples."

Danny was silent for a moment. "Why can't you tell me your idea?"

"The less you know, the better. Plausible deniability, right? Keep taking care of business, and I'll help as best I can from the sidelines."

Danny reached across and placed his hand on Eva's. "Whatever you're doing, I trust you. Just don't get yourself killed, okay?"

Eva smiled but didn't respond. She opened the truck door and stepped out on her wobbly legs.

"Sure you don't need help getting checked in?" Danny asked.

"I wish, but I don't want us spotted together on any cameras. That could send this whole thing crashing down. Just worry about you, okay? Pretend I'm dead. I'll see you around."

She closed the door and limped away to the motel's main office.

Danny drove off and parked at a Burger King a half-mile down the road. He pulled out his burner phone, the one the authorities still hopefully didn't know about.

Finding the name he desired from his original burner, he dialed the number and waited for the phone in South America to pick up.

"Gutierrez," the man answered.

"Gabe the babe! It's Danny Cortez from the U.S. How are you doing?"

"Danny?" Gabe replied, surprise filling the line. "How long's it been? Five years?"

Danny didn't mistake the sheer excitement in Gabe's voice. "Five long years. Man, time really flies, huh?"

Danny had worked with Gabriel Gutierrez five years prior on a case with the DEA. Danny had to locate the influential leaders of a drug cartel based out of Lima, Peru, in cooperation with the country's similar agency, the DEVIDA. Gutierrez lived in Lima and had served as an unofficial partner and tour guide during Danny's ten-month stay in the Peruvian capital.

The two men had developed a friendship over their love of soccer and often got together outside of work to watch games.

"Time does fly, my friend. I've got a wife and a little two-year-old girl," Gabe said. "Life's been changing for me, but I'm still out there hunting the bad guys."

"Congratulations, Gabe. Really happy for you. We'll need to catch up another time, though. I'm having some serious issues and could use your help."

"Something in Peru?"

"Not exactly. And my target isn't a cartel, or even drug dealers." Danny paused, considering how to phrase this next bit. "It's a United States senator."

"Senator? I don't know, Danny. My department would never pursue an American politician. That could cause all kinds of problems between our countries."

"I understand. And I'm not even asking you to pursue anything. But if you verify what I'm about to tell you, all I'm asking is you leak the story to your local press. We just need word to spread about this senator. We're working on the same thing here, but it's not as straightforward."

Gabe was silent for a moment. "Okay, Danny. Tell me."

Danny told him everything about the corruption within the U.S. and how it all tied back to Calloway. After speaking for nearly five minutes, filling in all the details swimming around in his head, Danny paused and let Gutierrez speak.

"Doesn't sound like I'll need to search much," Gabe said. "I can't get to it right this second, but give me until later tonight, okay? We've got to get your mother away from those guys."

"This is such a huge favor, Gabe. I don't know how to ever repay you."

"You'd do the same for me. That's all I need to know. And Danny, don't worry. Your name won't be mentioned in anything we share with the press."

Danny's other burner phone rang. An incoming call from Steele. His heart sank. "I'm sorry, Gabe, that's my other line ringing. It's them."

"Say no more, amigo. We'll talk very soon."

They hung up and Danny picked up the call from Steele without speaking.

"He escapes car bombs, cartels, and burned-down cabins," Steele said. "How does he do it?"

"Good morning, Mr. Steele. I'm sorry to say you only killed Eva Ramirez, which I assume was your goal. Considering my name isn't on that list."

Steele laughed. "Your name is not on *that* list. But it's on other lists. That's not what I'm calling about, though, Danny. We can get to that topic in a minute."

"What's so pressing? And how did you know I'm alive?"

"Just had someone stop by the hiking trail and he said your truck was gone. Not exactly an area known for theft, so we assumed you escaped. As you did. As far as this call, it's about your mother."

Danny sat bolt upright. "What have you done to her?"

"Nothing. But she suffered an incident last night. Started harming herself. I'll be sending you a picture of her. She's okay now. Bandaged up. But Danny, we need to come to an agreement. Because your mother's time is running out."

CHAPTER TWENTY-SIX

"AN AGREEMENT?" Danny asked. He rolled down his truck windows as the morning grew warmer. The Burger King parking lot had only three other cars. The rush would come later for lunch.

"Tell me something, Danny," Steele said. "Why were you shacked up with the Ramirez girl in that cabin? Did she make you fall for her that fast? I always thought you were more of a professional."

Eva had left Danny with some memorable words during their discussion in the cabin. They were all in an intense game of chess, where life and death were the only likely outcomes. "She was tough. I can't lie. See, part of my method is to build trust with my targets first. They let their guards down. That's why Vance let me into his house. We connected over our time in the DEA. Once that trust is built, I just need an opportunity to make my move."

"That seems like it could take some time."

"It didn't with Vance. But with Ramirez, she wouldn't budge. She had her own theories about everything going on. I had to tell her we were being watched on her front porch, and that's the only reason she let me inside. I had no chance of killing her at home. She could take me if it came down to it. I got lucky when your goons showed up. She had no other choice but to trust me."

Steele grunted. "And you killed two of them. I'll admit, Cortez, I had my doubts about you. Still do. Maybe that's just my trust issues.

You never know who you can trust when you're constantly dealing in this dark underworld of crime. Everyone has an agenda. Enough about my therapy issues, tell me about this cabin."

Danny hesitated before speaking again. Were Steele's words his own attempt to build trust with Danny? Last he checked, Steele planned to have Danny eliminated as well. "I found that deserted cabin in the woods several years ago. Back when I lived out here and would go on hikes. Always thought it was the perfect hideout. No one else ever ventured far enough off the trail to find it."

"I believe it," Steele said. "Once we pinpointed your location, we researched the property. It'd been there since the 1850s. Was used to house escaped slaves from the south. Provide them shelter and food before they traveled further north. Quite spectacular, really."

"Thanks for the history lesson. But I thought taking Ramirez there would allow her to relax just enough for me to strike. I planned on doing it this morning. Was going to chop some wood for a fire and make an errant swing to her head. But once again, your guys had to come and ruin it all. Was I supposed to die in that fire, too?"

Steele giggled. "Did she scream, Danny? What did she sound like?"

This is a truly sick man.

"Her scream woke me up," Danny said, letting the lies flow like water. "But it was too late. The cabin was filled with smoke, and I couldn't even see my hand in front of my face. If I tried to save her, we would've both ended up dead. I escaped and had to watch the cabin burn to the ground."

"That's quite the story, Danny. I'd apologize, but we got the result we wanted. Your death would have been a fortunate collateral. But you're here, and you can still be an asset to our cause."

"Don't jerk me around, Steele. The only reason you're calling is because my mom is failing. If she passes, you no longer have leverage over me. At that point, what reason would I have to not spill all of this corruption to the press?"

"Very good, Danny. You understand how negotiations work. Mind you, we still have all the leverage. We have the medicine that will keep your mother calm and comfortable. Should you not do as we ask, we'll withhold that medicine. The team looking after your mother assured me that would be catastrophic for her. Strapped to her bed so she can't hurt herself. Ever since we told her you're dead, she's really been spiraling. Like she's allowing the dementia to win."

Danny seethed. "That wasn't necessary, and you know it. Blatant cruelty."

"Maybe unnecessary, but a warning shot. And here we are. Next name on the list is Amber Williamson. She's on the other side of D.C. in Baltimore. We can have her schedule sent to you in the next five minutes. What's it going to be, Danny Boy?"

He hated when people called him that. Almost as much as he hated the song that had been remade a gazillion times.

"Keep my mother alive, you dirtbag. I'll head to Baltimore first thing in the morning."

CHAPTER TWENTY-SEVEN

THE SUN BEAMED through the thin excuse of a curtain hanging over Danny's motel window.

After hanging up with Steele, Danny headed to the opposite side of Fredericksburg and found a motel to spend the day and night. After a quick stop at a Wal-Mart to buy fresh clothes and toiletries, Danny would no longer risk public exposure. He remained in his room with a motel phone to order a pizza for lunch, enjoying the leftovers for dinner.

Not the best nutritional choice, but his top priority was sleep. He snoozed away the afternoon, watched TV for a couple of hours after dinner, then crashed for the rest of the night until the sun woke him in the morning.

He rolled out of bed with a newfound energy. And confidence.

Having left both phones off, Danny powered on the one Steele knew about and sent him a message.

> Send proof my mom is okay, and I'll head to Baltimore now.

He was done taking orders from this psychotic loon and would stand up for his end of the deal. If his mother was their leverage, then he wouldn't proceed with any agreement until his terms were met first. And that meant a healthy mom on her meds to ease the worsening dementia symptoms.

The extended shuteye rejuvenated Danny. He whistled random tunes while showering, taking his sweet time in the steam, and while he got ready for the day ahead. Things were finally in motion. Gabe was handling matters in Peru. And Eva was up to…something. Hopefully, Vance continued to keep his head in the sand.

He considered checking in with Nadia and Zak but wouldn't risk exposing their involvement at this point. He trusted both of them to find a safe way to expose the corruption to the American press.

After running to the motel lobby to grab an orange and a banana nut muffin for breakfast, Danny returned to his room and turned on the TV. He dropped his muffin and caught it mid-air when he read the headline on the news station.

SEN. CALLOWAY UNDER INVESTIGATION.

"What?" Danny shouted. He placed his breakfast items on his nightstand and paced around the room with his hands crossed behind his head. He blasted the volume, not wanting to miss a word.

The news anchor, a woman based in Richmond, spoke directly into Danny's soul. "Senator Richard Calloway of Louisiana has not been charged with any crimes. But the senate is launching a special committee to investigate his involvement in an alleged drug ring operation out of South America. A Peruvian news station first reported the story last night, claiming Senator Calloway has been overseeing an operation with the CIA to funnel drug profits back to his own pockets, all while eliminating dangerous drug cartels and their leaders."

"Gabe." Danny couldn't remove the grin stuck on his face. "You did it. You actually did it!"

"The Associated Press reached out to the senator's office for a quote, to which they replied, 'Senator Calloway is disturbed by these allegations against him by the Peruvian press and maintains his innocence.'"

"I'm sure you do." Danny cackled as the screen changed from the anchor and showed clips of the senator walking the halls of the Capitol building.

The anchor continued. "In a late-night post on social media, the senator appeared disturbed." The news channel then ran a clip, where Calloway scowled at the press, saying, "This is a smear campaign. Fake news. Shame on the Peruvian press for publishing such utter nonsense. Once my name is cleared, which it will be, I won't rest until I find the culprit behind these lies. Justice will be served."

Danny fell on the bed and howled with laughter. "You tell 'em, Senator!"

He wanted to call everyone and tell them to watch the news. This entire conspiracy would collapse in on itself soon enough. A Senate committee investigation didn't waste anyone's time. They wouldn't have launched the committee unless they believed the allegations had serious merit.

Danny checked his phone and found no response from Steele, although the instructions for Amber Williamson had come through last night while Danny slept.

"Amber," Danny muttered, "you get to live. We all get to live. Calloway will be behind bars along with all his accomplices. And we can return to a life of peace."

Danny returned his attention to the TV for more positive news.

Senator Bill Whitehorse from New Mexico spoke via a phone call with the news station. "We saw the news out of Peru, and I immediately hosted a call with some fellow senators on both sides of the aisle. While we believe in innocence until proven guilty, the accusations are too serious to ignore. With the help of a special Senate committee, which we plan to finalize this week, we hope to reach a swift decision on whether charges should be filed against Senator Calloway. I've already spoken with a handful of independent investigators who used to work in the Department of Justice. Three have given verbal agreements to work on this case together. The last thing we want is a corrupt senator continuing to work within the U.S. government. Until official charges are brought, the senator can continue his work as normal."

Danny didn't agree with allowing a senator to continue their work under such accusations. But without a concrete verdict, he supposed it was only fair. The last thing Americans needed was their senators having the ability to prevent their colleagues from working because of verbal accusations.

Regardless, this was one step closer to Calloway's downfall. Danny lowered the volume, his excitement getting the best of him.

But he remained trapped in the motel room, unable to do anything about the news except wait. The committee wouldn't be finalized for a week, if that. Then the investigations would begin. And how long would that take? Something this serious could take months. And that was just the investigation. If they found any relevant evidence, the next phase would be a congressional hearing and trial. Then impeachment hearings.

These guys have plenty of time to cover their tracks. Or flee the country before investigations begin.

Danny's joyous mood quickly dissipated. None of this changed the danger his mother faced. No Senate Committee would free her. Or Vance.

He sighed and turned off the TV, staring at his reflection in the black screen.

It's still up to me.

CHAPTER TWENTY-EIGHT

ACROSS FREDERICKSBURG, Eva sat in a silent motel room.

After Danny had dropped her off, she took a ninety-minute nap to help get her mind right. When she woke up, her legs still throbbed, but the height of the pain had subsided thanks to the Tylenol she purchased from the motel lobby's kiosk of travel necessities.

After taking a couple more pills, she jumped right into work, figuring out the details of her plan.

She had seen the news, which made her plans somewhat easier. All she needed was a ride to D.C.

Not normally one for backing up her work, Eva was glad she'd decided long ago to back up everything for the notes and documents she'd gathered about the CIA's involvement with the illegal operations in South America.

Eva spent time in the motel's business center—a single old desktop computer stationed in the lobby. It took a few minutes to power up, but the internet connection was strong enough to access her documents and add final notes about how it all tied to Senator Calloway.

She reviewed her documents at least five times, checking for inconsistencies that could fail in court. She had sat in enough trials to see evidence attacked by savvy attorneys. But Calloway wouldn't be so lucky. Eva had a record of emails send from Calloway to her colleagues in the CIA. All messages were intentionally vague, but she had access to her colleagues' responses to tie it all together, painting Calloway as the one giving orders.

Once it was cleaned up, she printed the fifty pages, earning curious glances from the front desk girl.

Eva asked, "Do you have an envelope I can keep these papers in?"

The girl behind the desk wore a University of Mary Washington shirt, the college in town. She rolled her eyes before settling them on Eva and reaching under the desk without breaking eye contact. She fished out a nine by twelve brown envelope, complete with a clasp to seal it shut.

"Anything else?" she asked in an irritated voice.

"I know your job isn't fun, and you just need it to pay for school, but try caring. You'll go a lot further in life if you can just pretend to care about what you're doing."

The girl frowned. "Excuse me, lady? You can't talk to me like that."

Eva grinned. "I was once in your position. Working a job I hated in college. Your approach is everything. Remember, this job isn't forever. Put some effort into it, and good things will come back around."

The girl laughed. "And you must be crushing life right now, staying at this cheap fleabag motel."

Eva could have told her off. Mentioned how she had been a successful CIA agent. A woman in a male-dominated field. Or the half a million dollars sitting in her savings account because of wise investments. But she bit her tongue. "Have a great day."

With the documents in hand, Eva had no choice but to power on her cell phone and call for a ride to the United States Capitol. Fifty-three miles was a pricey Uber, but she didn't care. Within the week, money would no longer matter to Eva. Whatever remained in her savings account would go to her mother.

When the Uber arrived, Eva rode with her head pressed against the window in the backseat. Her mother had raised her as best she could, but they'd had a rocky relationship. Dad had always been gone on work trips, which eventually resulted in an affair and divorce. He moved across the country and left Eva and her mother to fend for themselves.

She hadn't spoken to her father in at least twenty years.

But her mother? It had been a little over a year. They'd never seen eye to eye. Mom would always judge. The people Eva dated. What sports she played in high school. Eventually, they'd had a falling out when Eva expressed her desire to join the CIA.

Her mother's worries had come from a place of concern. She didn't want her only daughter caught up in danger all around the globe. But that had never taken away from the love. Her mother had always put food on the table and even eventually supported her in joining the CIA. The woman had also saved enough to take the two of them on a vacation every summer, despite their consistent fighting on every one.

So much fighting.

Nowadays, they only spoke once a year because it resulted in less arguing. If they connected any more than that, her mother would dredge up the past and they'd end up in a shouting match.

Finally, Eva couldn't take the drama anymore and made the tough decision to cut her mother out of her life.

It had been a tearful conversation when she'd delivered the news. One met by her mother not with rage, but regret. She'd understood her role in Eva's harsh choice and only protested once.

Since that night, they no longer spoke or visited each other on holidays or birthdays. No random messages. Their infrequent calls were only clerical. When Eva needed a copy of her birth certificate. Or when asking for her mother's social security number to designate her as a beneficiary since she had no one else.

It was the messiest part of Eva's life. One that kept her awake some nights, wondering if she had done the right thing. Neither woman ever made a move to open the lines of communication again. Eva viewed that as a sign they'd both found peace without each other. And peace was all anyone ever needed.

"Excuse me?" Eva spoke to her driver for the first time. "What day is it?"

"Today is Sunday," the man responded without even glancing in the rearview. He had equally kept to himself and listened to Spanish music at a low volume.

"Dammit. I'm sorry to do this, but I need to change the address we're going to."

The Capitol was closed on Sundays.

"No problem," he said. "Just change it on the app, and it'll change for me."

"Okay. It'll be a little closer in Arlington."

Eva had suspected she'd lose her job three months before it actually happened. After the first verbal warning from her superior, she'd started backing up her research documents. Besides those, she'd also backed up contact lists, schedules, and other information the U.S. government would deem highly illegal for her to take to her personal accounts.

That's why, regardless of how everything played out today, she would either get arrested or killed for her actions. Her money was on the latter.

Eva pulled up a private folder on her phone and searched through a massive list of congressmen and women, senators, aides, heads of departments, and everything in between.

She had no idea if Senator Whitehorse was on her list, but she breathed a sigh of relief when he was. Most senators, except for the few who finagled their way into becoming multi-millionaires, lived in Arlington.

Whitehorse was no different. A humble man from New Mexico who had campaigned with zero backing from mega donors or corporations.

Eva changed the address in the Uber app and watched the time to her final destination shrink from thirty minutes to twenty-one.

A hot flash struck her as nerves paraded through her body.

Eva dialed her mother, and the call went to voicemail. She drew in a deep breath before speaking. "Hi, Mom. It's me. I just wanted to call and see how you're doing. It's been a while. I hope you're okay."

Eva's voice cracked, tears rolling down her cheeks.

"I'm sorry for cutting you out of my life. I hope you can understand why I needed to do it. If only we could have had a healthier relationship, I know things would have been different. But you were right, Mom. This job is dangerous. But I don't regret it. It allowed me to travel the world. Do incredible things and meet even more incredible people. I just wish I'd had you in my corner through it all.

"I'm not calling to dwell on the past. Pretty sure we've both spent plenty of our days doing that. I'm proud of the mom you are. You raised me into the woman I am today. No one else can claim that. It was all you. You can smile now. Because when I leave this world, it will be as a hero. I don't know how the news coverage will be—if there'll be any—but never doubt I went out doing the right thing to make the world a better place. I love you."

Eva hung up, tears pouring out. Now the driver glanced at her in the rearview, his eyes darting from the mirror to the road every two seconds. But he didn't say a word as they exited the highway in Arlington and drove through upper-class neighborhoods.

With each passing block, dread and excitement bubbled within Eva. The pain in her legs lessened. Likely because of the adrenaline overflowing in her veins.

The car came to a stop on the curb outside of a white ranch-style home. "We're here, miss."

"Thank you. Keep the car running, I'm gonna need a ride back to the motel."

Eva stepped out of the car, envelope tucked under her arm, and strode up to the door of Senator Bill Whitehorse.

CHAPTER TWENTY-NINE

DANNY NEVER HEARD from Steele after his request for proof of his mother's life.

Still, he traveled to Baltimore on Sunday night and checked into a new motel. Steele would send something to show Tatiana was still alive and well, but the corrupt DEA leader had likely spent his Sunday in a state of panic after the news about Senator Calloway had broken. How long would it be until Steele's name surfaced as an accomplice?

So many fires to put out for poor ol' Steele.

Danny enjoyed another deep sleep into Monday morning, waking in an energized state of mind. The motel was an upgrade from the last, considering they had a waffle iron included with their continental breakfast offerings. With no plans for the day ahead, aside from locating Amber Williamson and verifying her daily schedule, Danny enjoyed his waffle and muffin in the motel's dining area.

An older man sat at one table, sipping from a cup of coffee. He watched the TV hanging in the room's corner, its volume blasting a shampoo commercial. The two nodded at each other as Danny sat down at the other table and dug into his meal.

The commercials ended and returned to CNN, where a panel of political analysts discussed the unfolding details about Senator Calloway.

They had nothing but speculation to argue about. One analyst claimed Calloway represented everything wrong with the current political climate. While his counterpart urged everyone to withhold their opinions until a prosecutor presented evidence.

"Quite the story." The other man gestured to the TV, putting his coffee cup down and chuckling. "Have you been following it?"

Danny swallowed a bite of waffle and set down his fork. "I've heard bits. What do you think's going on?"

"A corrupt politician? Never had a hard time believing that. Most of them are in it to improve their own lives. They don't care about the people they serve. Why do you think so many of them retire as millionaires?"

Danny nodded along. "I have to agree. We have plenty of issues with our system of government, but I like to think the checks and balances hold up well enough."

The man raised his coffee cup. "I'll drink to that. This investigation and potential trial will be a solid test of those checks." He chuckled again and placed the mug to his lips. "We shall see."

"Always keep the faith," Danny said. "That's all we can do."

The man grinned and took a sip of coffee. Danny stood and fished a bottle of orange juice out of the mini fridge on the counter and sat back down.

The news coverage changed, accompanied by a dramatic audio stinger and red graphics flashing across the screen to indicate breaking news. The feed cut away from the panel and showed a middle-aged anchor named Brian Crawford.

"We have breaking news out of Washington. A former CIA agent was found murdered this morning in a motel in Fredericksburg, Virginia. We turn to CIA Director, John Ellis, live in the CIA's press briefing room."

The screen cut to a man with a chiseled jaw standing behind a podium, sorrow plastered on his face.

"Good morning. It is with great regret I announce the murder of Eva Ramirez, a former agent of the CIA."

Danny choked on his first sip of orange juice and gulped more down to clear his throat. A photo of Eva flashed on the screen. Her official government photo, in which she carried a stern expression.

"No," Danny whispered to himself.

"In her time with the agency, Ms. Ramirez worked on several covert operations in the Middle East, Africa, Central and South America. Her cases were highly classified, but her record speaks for itself. Because of Ms. Ramirez, some of the most dangerous terrorists and organized crime members are behind bars. She made the world a safer place, and we forever owe her a debt of gratitude."

Danny stood up from his seat, glaring at the TV. The old man eyed him and arched a brow. "You okay, young man? Did you know that woman?"

"I..." Danny began but wasn't sure what exactly to say. "I've worked with her before. Didn't know her too well but always heard good things."

The man shook his head. "It's a damn shame that the people who keep the world safe are the ones who get murdered. I suppose that's a risk of the job, but that don't make it any easier to accept when these things happen."

Danny licked his lips while the CIA director explained how Eva was found shot to death in her motel room.

While the public gobbled up every word coming out of the director's mouth, Danny questioned it all.

Eva had been alone at her motel, and from what Danny could tell, she didn't have a wide network of friends or family who would check in with her regularly. So, who found her? Who thought to look?

Of course, the motel staff could have gone in for their daily routines, but Eva would've made sure no one entered her room. Danny doubted she would've been surprised by something as simple as a knock on the door.

She had mentioned an idea about their predicament and how to get out of it. Had she already executed those plans? Danny doubted she could have made any serious moves in the short time since he'd left her at the motel, but nothing else explained why those criminals would have murdered her.

It was them.

Danny refused to believe any other theory.

The CIA director actually went on TV to praise the work Eva had once done for them. Danny balled his hands into fists. How he wanted to pulverize all of these sick people. And to shower compliments on Eva, all while being involved with the illegal operation that ordered her execution made Danny's blood boil.

Asshole.

Aside from the obvious rage brewing, Danny understood the hit list he was supposed to be working on was no longer in his hands.

They had gone out of their way to burn them alive in the middle of the woods. They'd believed Eva was dead for a moment, but once they learned otherwise, they pounced to remove her from the world without hesitation.

John Ellis finished his prepared statement, faking some tears for added theatrics. The press pool erupted with questions. He pointed to a single reporter, quieting the room.

"Director Ellis, do you believe the murder was done as revenge by someone with ties to the criminals Ms. Ramirez helped put in prison?"

"That's where our investigations will begin," Ellis said. "We have a team working with the motel to pull any video coverage they might have. Initial reports suggest a black van pulled up to the motel minutes before Ms. Ramirez's death. Whoever was in the van never checked in and left a few moments after their arrival."

"License plates, or anything the public can help with identifying?"

"Not yet. I expect more details by the end of the day, and we'll share them with you."

Danny balled his fists with each word that came out of this liar's mouth. Ellis could have killed Eva himself. He certainly had the resources to alter video footage. Or disappear altogether.

He needed to find Amber Williamson today and warn her. The gloves were off, and he no longer trusted Steele or his cronies to allow him to execute his plans. If she wasn't dead by the time they required, they'd deal with it directly.

I need to call Zak. His name is next on the list, after Amber.

Danny had shown the list to Zak and trusted his friend to hide. This wouldn't surprise Zak, but his friend needed to prepare for whatever these criminals might throw his way. Maybe going into the CIA offices was his safest bet. They wouldn't dare orchestrate a murder in the middle of a government building. Right?

He powered on his cell phone, the secret one, and waited as several notifications popped up. Missed text messages from Eva. She had reached out to him and never received a response.

His stomach sank. She could have been alive right now. They could have fled to a different state. But after reading the messages, his worries eased. She hadn't reached out for help. Only to inform.

EVA

The documents are with the right person.
Expect some fireworks this week.

Not counting on many days to live.

Keep going forward. We're so close.

Danny squeezed his phone. She knew she was going to die?

Her vague message opened up a flood of questions. None of which Danny had time to ponder, because when he stared up at the TV again, every drop of blood froze in his veins.

"We do have one person of interest, and we believe he is still in the D.C. area. In fact, he was last seen with Ms. Ramirez near a hiking trail north of Fredericksburg."

Staring back was a portrait of himself. An older, official portrait of his days with the DEA.

"His name is Daniel Cortez. And if you spot him, know he is armed and dangerous."

CHAPTER THIRTY

DANNY RETURNED TO HIS ROOM, a sickening sensation growing in his stomach. The room spun around him, his vision going in and out of focus.

Did the CIA director really just speak his name on live television? And suggest his involvement with Eva's death?

Danny dodged a bullet with the elderly man not making the connection to who sat across from him. Granted, the picture they displayed showed a younger Danny with more scruff and facial hair.

He had calls to make and refused to place them from the motel. Steele had eyes all over him, and Danny had to throw him off his true location.

He hopped in his truck and drove fifteen minutes east to a different motel parking lot and dialed Steele first.

"I've been expecting your call," Steele answered. "You saw our guy on TV, I presume?"

"What kind of game is this?" Danny asked. "I thought you wanted me to work on this list of names. You claimed you could protect me, cover my tracks. Instead, my face is plastered all over the news. How can I assassinate someone with a target already on my back? I'm thinking our professional relationship is coming toward its end. You clearly have no problem leaving me out for dead."

Steele laughed. "In my defense, I had no idea Ellis planned to do that. He was supposed to deliver his remarks, praise your lady friend, and field a few questions."

"Okay, so I'll go after him first then. But what's his angle?" Danny forced all the sass he could muster into his tone. "Did he not know I'm trying to help you people?"

"He's aware of your role in our operation. Haven't had a chance to speak with him. Hasn't picked up my calls. But don't worry, Cortez, he can clear your name and make it all disappear with a simple statement."

"You better hope so. Because I'm not doing a damn thing until that happens."

"Yes, yes, that's why I've been trying to get hold of him. I knew that would be your response."

"You're backing me into a corner, Steele. Even before any of this happened. Not feeling the trust after you set the cabin on fire where I slept."

Steele sighed. "We trusted you'd survive."

"No, you said I'd have been a fortunate collateral."

"It was a win-win for us. Speaking of trust, you think you get to skate free after lying about the Ramirez girl? Died in the fire, huh? She never even changed her phone after the CIA fired her. The second she turned it on we had eyes on her." Steele chuckled. "Tell me, Cortez, were you actually going to kill her? Or did you develop feelings that quickly? Alone with a woman at a cabin in the woods. How could it not be romantic?"

"Fine." Danny changed his tone and approach. No more chess games. Stroke the ego of his mother's captor. That never failed. "Yes, I planned to kill her. But after the fire, she *was* seriously injured. Couldn't even walk. I showed her mercy. She was in excruciating pain and refused a hospital. Honestly, I thought she would die on her own. She might have, too, if your goons had just left her alone."

Steele chuckled. "Oh, Daniel. She played you, man. She wasn't hurt."

"I saw it with my own eyes," Danny said. "A log from the ceiling smashed her. She was unconscious most of the night."

"Well, she wasn't hurt enough to take a trip to Arlington and stop by Senator Whitehorse's personal residence."

Heat flushed Danny's face. What the hell had Eva been up to? "Whitehorse? What was she doing there?"

"I was hoping you could tell me."

Danny thought back to her text message. Perhaps the last one she ever sent.

The documents are with the right person.

Was Whitehorse that person? Considering the circumstances, nothing else made sense. Whitehorse had been on TV speaking about the accusations against Calloway. Eva took a chance and delivered whatever documents she had to his house.

"She never mentioned anything about him," Danny said. "Do you know how long she was at his house?"

"According to the Uber records, no more than a minute. She had a ride from Fredericksburg there and back. Maybe she went to speak with him, and he wasn't home. We're not sure. We've submitted a request to the senator's office for more details, if he was even aware of her visit. He has a camera doorbell, so we're hoping that will provide us insight."

"Interesting. You've tracked her every move since leaving the cabin? Considering how in tune you are with what we're all doing, tell me, Steele, how long did it take for you to pinpoint my current location after I called?"

"I'm not hiding anything, Cortez. We need to know where everyone is at all times. We lost you for a few hours. Been keeping your phone off?"

"Of course. It's none of your business where I am."

"That's where you're wrong," Steele said, his voice rising. "You're currently at the Rodeway Inn, and we trust you'll remain there until Ms. Williamson is dead."

"Get my face off the news and I'll proceed. Until then, you can kill her yourselves."

"Now, now, Danny, let's not be unreasonable. We're on the same team. You keep forgetting that. And you shouldn't turn your phone off. What if we need to contact you about your mother?"

"I'll do things my way," Danny said. "Thanks."

Danny hung up and turned off the burner phone, fuming from Steele's mention of his mother. *How dare they keep her as bait.*

He powered on his second burner and dialed Nadia. After five rings, she answered.

"Danny?" she answered, breathing heavy. "Tell me it's really you?"

"It's me. Why do you sound like you're in a panic?"

"Why do *you* think, Danny?! You haven't reached out in days! Then, your picture was on the news. They're saying you killed that woman. Zak assured me you didn't."

"Okay, slow down. First off, I take it Zak is okay?"

"Oh, you're worried about *him* and not *me*?" Danny recognized Nadia's tone from the final months of their former relationship. God help anyone who defied Nadia in her current mental state. "He's fine. Did you want to speak with him?"

"Yes."

White noise filled Danny's ear as she passed the phone over.

"Hey, Dan. Glad you're still okay. What's going on with you?"

"Where are you, Zak?"

"At home. Why?"

"You both need to leave. They're no longer leaving the assassinations to me. They found the cabin and burned it to the ground. We were asleep inside but made it out. Eva's really dead, though. *They* shot her in her motel room."

"I figured as much," Zak said. "Surprised you weren't with her at the time."

"She insisted on being alone. Said she was going to make moves. I think she gave some documents to Senator Whitehorse. But I'm not sure what exactly."

"Where should we go?"

"It doesn't matter. Just turn off your phone. Computer. Anything they can use to track you. Don't use credit cards. Have Nadia withdraw cash from the bank and use that to get around. Hop around somewhere different every night. And if you must turn your phone on, do it away from where you're staying. That's how they found Eva. That's how they found me."

"Okay, I hear you, Dan." Worry crept into Zak's voice. "Give me two minutes to grab some things and we'll be out of here. Here's Nadia."

Zak passed the phone back to Nadia.

"He's right, Danny. We'll hide, but we're not leaving town. Enough with rolling over to these goons. We need to fight."

"Aren't you supposed to be back in Chicago today for work?" Danny asked.

"I called out for the week. This is too important, Danny. Zak and I have been hard at work, hacking into all kinds of government systems to see what we can find."

Danny's stomach fluttered. Even after all of Nadia's resistance to help. Her flat out denial. She still had his back. Just like he would always have hers. "Never expected you to extend your stay."

"You know I love your mom, Danny. I guess my inner prosecutor really wants to see these fools brought to justice. My boss isn't pleased, but I assured her I'll have a hell of a story when I get back. And who knows, maybe this will all lead to me getting a job back here in D.C." She paused a moment. "I can't lie, I've enjoyed being back out here."

Danny wouldn't mind moving back to D.C. either. But could he, if Nadia did the same?

He'd had enough of the mind games. Between Nadia and Steele, Danny dreaded how they both kept him guessing. Nadia, with the ever-changing emotions of insisting their relationship was dead, but dropping random lines reminiscing about her time in Washington. *Their* time. And Steele, who kept toeing the line between wanting Danny to kill *and* be killed.

"Oh my God!" Zak shouted in the background. "I got it! And it's there! Give me the phone."

The ruffle of the phone being snatched out of Nadia's hand preceded Zak's panting voice.

"Dan. I got in. I know where they're keeping your mom."

CHAPTER THIRTY-ONE

DANNY HAD ONLY HEARD of Sandtown, one of the roughest neighborhoods in Baltimore.

Sure, he was delighted to learn he was in the same city as his mother. But he had to go through a crime-ridden area to find her. Without a gun.

Block after block, Danny passed abandoned homes and commercial buildings. Graffiti on the walls. Bars over the shattered windows. Litter up and down the streets.

He drove into the neighborhood, avoiding the abandoned warehouse in which his mother was being held. The government criminals must have found a unique opportunity to house their hostages in a part of town no one would dare look. And the rent would be either dirt-cheap or nonexistent.

A liquor store on the corner had a crowd of men standing outside, several smoking cigarettes or joints. The scent made him crave some sweet reefer, but that would have to wait as a celebration for reuniting with his mother. He parked along the curb and stepped out of his truck, approaching the group of six men. They each watched him with undivided attention.

The man closest to Danny gripped a bottle of Crown Royal by the neck and took a swig before speaking, liquor dribbling from the corner of his mouth. "What you want, man? You not from around here."

Danny raised his hands in a peaceful gesture. "I need a gun. Was told I could find one here."

This is as good a chance as any. Hopefully, these guys don't get offended by my assumptions.

The man took another sip from the bottle and glanced over at his friends. Another man leaning against the building pushed off and approached, plucking the cigarette out of his lips and blowing a plume of smoke into Danny's face.

"Who told you that?" he asked, stepping within six inches of Danny. His breath reeked of booze and tobacco. Danny studied the several cracks on the man's pale lips, wondering what other drugs he may do regularly.

"Just the guy at the gas station. Told me to come to the liquor store," Danny said. "Am I at the wrong place? Didn't mean to cause you fellas any trouble."

The man rubbed his crusty lips and took a step back. "No, you at the right spot. Just makin' sure you ain't no punk ass pig."

"No, just need to take care of someone."

The man studied him, peering into Danny's eyes. Danny had witnessed enough interrogations to understand the eyes could never lie. Reading someone else's though? That's where the challenge came into play.

"What gun you looking for?" the man asked, apparently deciding Danny had passed his internal test.

"Something easy to pack," Danny said. "I prefer Glocks."

The man glanced at another in the group, who nodded in response before disappearing into the liquor store.

"Give Dee a minute to get what you're looking for. Will be two hundred with ammo. One fifty without."

"I'll need the ammo."

The man took another drag from his cigarette and pointed the burning tip at Danny. "Who's causing you problems? Darryl or Baby?"

"I'm not even sure exactly who I'm looking for. Just that they'll be at an abandoned warehouse on Ninth Street."

The man frowned. "The old furniture factory? That building's been empty for twenty years. I walk by it every day. Never seen nobody go in or out."

Danny shrugged. "That's all I know. If I get there and it's empty, then I guess this was all for nothing. But I gotta go look."

"I know everything going on in this town, and I'm telling you that place is empty. Might find some bums camping out in there, but nothing else."

"I appreciate the heads up."

Dee stepped out of the liquor store with a black backpack slung over his shoulder. "Here you go, Tre." He handed it to the man talking to Danny and returned to his post against the wall.

Danny fished in his pocket for his wallet and pulled out a couple of hundred-dollar bills.

Tre peeked into the backpack. "Glock 42's all we got. You cool with that?"

It was one of the smaller Glocks in circulation. Kind of weak, but easy to conceal. "I'll take it."

Tre nodded and pulled it out, keeping it against his stomach while rubbing it down with a cloth. "Serial number's scratched off. If anyone asks, you didn't get it from here, understand?"

"Of course."

"The two bills."

Danny handed the cash over. Tre snatched it out of this grip and stuffed it into a pocket. He reached out with the Glock's grip facing Danny.

Danny grabbed the gun and tucked it into his waistband.

"It's already loaded," Tre said. "And here's another carton of ammo."

Danny took the box and dropped it into his back pocket. "Thank you."

"You let us know if you need anything else."

Danny nodded and spun around to return to his truck, all the men's eyes following him.

When he reached the side of his truck, a man jumped out of a vehicle parked eight car lengths further up the block.

He wore a dark blue jacket with sunglasses. At first glance, he appeared to be a government official. Could've been FBI or DEA.

The man dashed ten steps toward Danny and pulled a pistol from a holster on his hip. Reacting too late, Danny jumped behind his truck as the man opened fire. A round whizzed by Danny's flailing feet as he crashed to the ground, dirt filling his nostrils, arms scraping against the pavement.

The gunfire continued, sparking the men at the liquor store to shout and duck for cover inside the store. Moments later, they returned outside, each armed and opened fire on the man at the end of the block.

Danny peered around the back of his truck in time to see at least a dozen rounds peppered across the fed's body. He jerked and flailed around like he'd been electrocuted. The force of the bullets pushed him backwards and sent his dead body collapsing to the ground.

Danny sighed in relief, leaning against his truck to examine his arms. Blood oozed from several cuts, and he plucked out small rocks that had wedged into his flesh. The scrapes left a burning sensation that tingled with each arm movement.

The men from the liquor all sprinted toward the end of the block, huddling around the body.

Danny joined them.

"Who this?" one man asked.

"Did we just kill a fed?" Tre asked.

"Why did you shoot him?"

"We all shot him. Why did *he* shoot?"

The panic grew palpable.

"Let me take a look, gentlemen," Danny said, pushing through the crowd. "He was coming for me."

"You got feds coming after you?" Tre asked. "You thought we shouldn't know that part?"

"I told you I wasn't sure who I was after," Danny said. "Or who was after me."

Danny dropped to a knee, avoiding the pool of blood forming beneath the fed. He patted the man's pockets and pulled out his wallet. Inside was a bundle of single dollar bills, credit cards, and a driver's license. Danny pulled out the license and read the name Matthew Murray.

Danny kept patting down the man and finally found a badge inside his jacket pocket.

It glinted beneath the overcast sky, undeniable. CIA.

Danny blew out a long exhale and peered up at the men hovering above him.

"CIA?" one said, grabbing his head. "We just killed someone from the CIA?"

"Calm down," Danny said. "He's from the CIA, but he's crooked."

"They don't care about no crooked cops in court. All they see is one of their own murdered. Who did it. Where it happened." He swore under his breath and looked up at the sky. "We can't get locked up for this. Wasn't even our fault."

"Can you guys make this body disappear?" Danny asked.

"Of course we can. But that'd just make it worse for us."

Danny found a cell phone in Matthew Murray's other pocket and pulled it out, standing up. "Look guys, I can't go into too many details, but a lot of these feds are going down soon anyway. Hide this body. If anything comes back to you, I'll testify as a witness. You have my word."

"And who the hell are you that they'll care what you say?"

"I'm an ex-DEA agent."

The group of men backed away from him, muttering profanities to themselves.

"Ah, hell no! You told us you wasn't a cop."

"I'm not a cop, and I never was a cop. I'm not out here to give you guys trouble." Danny looked each man in the eye, silently willing them to understand. "These people kidnapped my mom, and I'm just trying to get her back. She's being held in that abandoned warehouse."

While the men argued amongst themselves, Danny dropped back down to use Murray's fingerprint to unlock the cell phone. He had several messages to both John Ellis and Charles Steele. Matthew Murray was deeply involved with both the CIA and DEA in their illegal operations.

Daily, in fact.

Murray appeared to work as the primary enforcer for these two men. He had orchestrated the attacks at Hotel Washington. He had been involved with the burning of the cabin, and the surveillance of Danny and Eva. Had even prepared the initial reports on Vance.

Danny took out his phone and snapped pictures of the messages that could be used as proof against these corrupt men. He texted them to Zak and started back to his truck. He didn't need to worry about being located in this precise moment—Danny was already headed to Calloway's turf.

"Where you going?" Tre called after him.

Danny glanced back over his shoulder. "Do whatever you need with the body. I'm getting my mom back."

CHAPTER THIRTY-TWO

"I DON'T KNOW about this, Zak," Nadia said. "This can all end up going horribly wrong for you."

Zak grinned. After he packed a suitcase with enough clothes for a week, they hopped in his car and drove into D.C. "They're all over Danny. We need to get them off his trail. Even if it splits them up, we'll call it a success. Besides, this should really crank the heat on the bigwigs. We've gotta cut these guys off at the head."

"And I don't disagree with that. But you could end up killed."

"I've already worked out all the details. We'll have an hour head start before the press releases what I'm sharing with them. If they even decide to. There's a lot of moving pieces."

When they arrived in the nation's capital, Zak drove them directly to the offices of the *Washington Post*. He had a friend who worked in the press pool with access to the Oval Office and several other government entities across the city. Zak had called her and requested a private press briefing about corruption within his DEA department. As one of the longer tenured employees at the DEA, his friend agreed to hear him out.

He parked in the underground garage and killed the engine, turning to Nadia. "I don't want you to come in with me. Yes, I know you helped with plenty of the research, but this isn't about credit."

Nadia rolled her eyes. "Then why am I here?"

"You're here because you're with me, and this is something I need to do. Obviously, if it was safe for you to stay at my house, we would have done that."

"And you want me to sit in this car and wait? Is it not safe inside this building? I don't see why I can't just come in."

Zak sighed. "The fewer people they know were involved with this, the better. If it leaked through the press that you were next to me during this press conference, we don't know what they will publish. It's best to stay off the radar as much as possible."

Nadia crossed her arms and leaned back in her seat, lips pursed. "Fine. I'll sit here and hope nothing happens to me."

Zak opened his door and stepped out, poking his head back in. "You're safe here. It's a garage under the city. I'll be back in an hour. Just hang tight. We need to do this if we ever want to live without fear again."

Zak closed the door and hurried toward the elevators, taking one to the building's main level for the lobby. He marched into the office building, admiring its modernized interior of glass walls, quotes in defense of the truth and democracy plastered around.

Hundreds of workers rushed through the building's lobby during the lunch rush hour.

Zak approached the welcome desk, where a college-aged man sat with a headset. He beamed as Zak approached, but the expression didn't meet his eyes. His nameplate read Drew Marsden.

"Good morning, sir," Drew said. "How can I help you?"

"I have an appointment with Erica Bertolli. My name is Zakary Larocque."

Drew nodded and turned his attention to his computer, typing what Zak presumed was a message to Erica. After a few minutes, Drew said, "She'll be right down, Mr. Larocque. Please take a seat."

He gestured toward the sofas behind Zak.

"Thank you."

Zak settled on the sofa and watched the people rotating through the lobby. Interns, political aides, journalists. Even a group taking a tour. He'd never done the touristy things like visiting the memorials and historical artifacts. He once went on a date at the Ford Theater where they shot Lincoln, but aside from the opera he had to endure, it was just a typical theater.

He waited only two minutes before Erica strode up.

"Zak?"

"Erica!" He rose with a wide grin and extended his arms for a hug. "So great to see you."

She hugged him back. "Same. How long's it been?"

Zak laughed. "I prefer not to think about how long ago college was. The crazy part is how we've been working in the same city, and I had no idea until recently. How've you been?"

"Loving this new job here," she said. "Been six months now. Hopped around over the last ten years. New York Times. The Atlantic. Now I'm here. Shall we head upstairs?"

Erica led him into the elevator lobby, and they took it up to the seventh floor. Zak caught her up with everything that had been going on in his life, aside from the juicy details he would soon present to her.

When they arrived on the seventh floor, the doors parted to a much quieter bullpen area. Journalists sat at their desks, eyes glued to their computer screens. Others were on the phone, speaking in hushed tones.

"It's like another world up here," Zak said.

Erica giggled. "This is where the serious work gets done. C'mon."

He followed her down another hallway, passing a cluster of offices with their doors closed. Zak fought the urge to enjoy the swish of Erica's hips while she strolled along. They'd had a fling back in their college days at Northeastern University in Boston. Nothing serious enough to make this reunion awkward, but enough to make Zak wonder about the age-old question. *What if?*

They reached the end of the hallway, and Erica pushed open a door labeled BRIEFING ROOM.

Inside, a table stood at the front of the room, facing several chairs. Only the chairs weren't empty. Seven journalists were scattered across the briefing room, all of whom rose to their feet upon their entrance.

Zak came to a halt, surveying the crowd around the room. This was not what he'd expected, nor what they'd discussed.

"What's all this?" he asked.

"Come in." Erica grinned and patted Zak on the back, guiding him toward the table at the front. "Have a seat."

He took a chair close to the door, in case he needed a quick escape. "Am I in some sort of trouble?"

Erica stood in front of Zak's table and faced the others in the room. "Thank you to everyone for making it over here on such short notice. This is Zakary Larocque. He currently works for the DEA and has been the unofficial number two under Administrator Steele. He comes to us with information about the suspicions we've had within the agency."

She turned to face Zak. "I wanted to tell you sooner, Zak, but thought it would be safest to deliver this news in person. We received a handful of tips a couple of months ago about this same topic. It led us to form a trustworthy, small group of journalists to investigate the allegations. We've been sitting on some vital intel and look forward to what you have to add.

"With the accusations against Senator Calloway this past weekend, we feel now is the most crucial time for our group to release a formal statement of our findings. Our hope is that whatever additional information you provide today will give us a complete picture of the happenings within the DEA since Administrator Steele took control.

"In this room, we have investigative journalists from the *New York Times, Los Angeles Times, Miami Herald, Chicago Tribune,* and of course, the *Washington Post*." She turned back to Zak, a sympathetic smile on her lips. "If you're ready to begin, the floor is all yours."

Anxiety flooded Zak's body. A slight tremble crept into his hands. This wasn't supposed to be a major press briefing in front of an audience. Zak had thought it would be a private conversation in Erica's office.

But apparently, this investigation had already been underway for some time.

Former DEA Administrator Alice Mildred's involvement restored some of Zak's faith in justice being served to those responsible. While he never reported directly to Mildred, she had taken him under her wing in the months before her departure. Maybe she'd already known then that Steele was corrupt and sought others to trust within the agency. But she'd mentioned nothing to Zak, only offering him career guidance.

One particular bit of advice stood out now, as Zak rose to stand at a podium next to the table. *Be ready to rise to the moment with no notice. It's those opportunities that separate the weak from the strong. Which will you be?*

And here was Zak, faced with his moment of reckoning. He could've protested the impromptu ambush by this press pool. But what good would that do? These people weren't here to argue with him. They chose to help. They were on the same team. If Zak cowered at this moment, the corruption would continue. Danny's mom would remain captive. And his best friend would stay running for his life everywhere he went.

Zak grabbed the sides of the podium and thanked everyone for joining him.

For the next twenty minutes, Zak spoke without interruption, telling them everything he had observed within the DEA offices, and everything he had found from hacking into their systems. He had to power on his cell phone to access his notes and found the new text message from Danny with new findings from a phone belonging to Matthew Murray of the CIA.

When Zak finished speaking, the entire press pool stood and showered him with a standing ovation. Erica approached him first, throwing her arms around his shoulders and squeezing him in a tight hug. With her lips nearly pressed against his ears, she said, "Zak, you've just ignited a full-on federal investigation."

CHAPTER THIRTY-THREE

AN INTERNAL CLOCK ticked inside Danny's head as he sat outside the fenced-off warehouse.

How much time did he have before word spread about Matthew Murray's death? Knowing how closely the CIA was monitoring everyone involved in their scheme—and considering Murray was Ellis' righthand man—Danny figured it would take less than four hours for them to understand something had gone wrong.

He should have told those men to dispose of Murray's cell phone before tossing his body in a lake, or whatever they planned to do. But his thoughts had rushed to his mother. Dealing with the body of a man who had just tried to kill him was more of a nuisance than a serious problem—considering he was only feet away from rescuing his mom.

The warehouse sat in a massive lot. The fencing around the property stood about a hundred feet away from the building. Warning signs hung from the fence in various spots, tattered, sun-bleached, and dangling from frayed wire.

Danny parked and got out of his truck, walking around the perimeter in search of the best way in. His small Glock snug in his waistband, Danny kept reaching back to ensure it remained there, ready for anyone who might shoot from the building. The property's main entrance faced the adjacent neighborhood. The old gate that had once allowed cars in and out remained closed with five different padlocks.

It wasn't until Danny reached the back side of the property that he found an area of fence torn apart just wide enough to allow a vehicle to drive through. His heart rate increased at the sight of a dozen cars parked behind the building.

This is it.

He remained at the fence to study the path in front of him. A row of windows on the second or third floor made it impossible to tell if anyone had eyes on him from such a distance away. A lone door stood open near the parked cars.

Danny pulled out his Glock, sliding his finger over the trigger. He could be met with more bullets, or perhaps the people inside the warehouse would have no idea who he was. He supposed reality was somewhere in the middle.

He strolled past the busted fence and marched up to the warehouse, confidence swirling. Having a definitive conclusion in sight always elevated his sense of purpose. Today, he would either leave the warehouse with his mother alive. Or leave in a body bag.

When he reached the parked cars, Danny crouched low to remain concealed behind them. Luxury cars mixed with more practical ones. Danny found refuge behind a shiny black Mercedes sedan.

Adrenaline crept into his veins. Danny's vision pulsed as he narrowed his focus on the door standing wide open.

They're hidden enough that they probably don't feel the need to have a guard patrolling the entryway. They had nothing like that at the other warehouse in Texas.

Danny debated if entering the warehouse with his gun visible was the best option. He'd need it if they greeted him with gunfire.

He kept the gun in hand but lowered to his side.

Danny stepped out from behind the Mercedes, remaining crouched, and inched his way toward the building. The open doorway appeared as a black hole in the building's facade. He hesitated as he approached, the lack of visibility into the building was frustrating.

A man dressed in all black charged out of the door and opened fire with an AR-15, the bullets spraying where Danny's head might have been if he'd been standing.

With nowhere to hide, Danny dropped to a knee and lined up a shot. He fired two rounds, and the man tumbled to the ground, blood drops trailing behind his last movements.

Danny raced to the dead man and grabbed his AR-15, pleased to find an extended magazine attached. He had at least twenty rounds available in the assault rifle, a boost to his confidence.

Voices shouted inside the warehouse. Danny waited, bracing for someone to barrel out of the doorway, but no one ever came. They wouldn't give him the advantage of mowing them down one-by-one.

I have to go in there. It doesn't end any other way.

Danny raced to the brick exterior wall about twenty feet from the open door. As he crept toward the entrance, the shouting from within grew louder. Inches from the door, Danny poked the muzzle of his rifle inside.

Three shots whizzed out of the doorway.

Quick to pull the trigger.

He did the same. In the absence of return fire, he somersaulted through the door and along the interior wall. Several rounds zinged over his head, giving Danny only seconds to examine his surroundings and find the safest route forward.

Tables were clustered to the left of the door. Open soda cans and water bottles remained scattered among half-eaten sandwiches.

I must have disrupted their lunch break.

To his right a metal locker stood against the wall. Danny dropped his shoulder into the side of it and lunged forward, knocking it over. Its contents spilled out across the floor. Jackets. Guns. Body armor.

A ballistic helmet spun on the floor. Danny snatched it, dropping it on his head as he dove behind the locker. The gunfire continued, shards of concrete from the floor and drywall flying in every direction.

He peered over the top of the locker, scanning the warehouse for more options. A stairwell waited fifty feet away to his right. The multiple floors were all open, leaving men shooting at him from high above. Thanks to his position against the wall, no one had a clean shot.

"Come out, Cortez!" a voice shouted. "We've got you cornered!

We've already called Steele to let him know you're here. You have no way out!"

Danny crawled to the end of the locker, peeking around the far edge. Six men were positioned on the ground level, all evenly spaced apart to form a semicircle around Danny. They remained thirty feet away, but kept closing in. If Danny waited any longer, they'd have him surrounded without a fight. The men from the higher floors were no longer there, and footsteps echoed from the stairwell.

With men closing around him, Danny jumped up and fired five rapid shots in the general direction of those he had just seen. He dropped back down before they responded.

"Walters!" someone shouted. "He shot Walters!"

Danny sensed the brief diversion and stood again. Two men dashed toward their colleague writhing on the ground. Danny pulled the trigger and swept the rifle across the two men, bullets smashing against their skulls. Both dropped to the floor.

Danny crouched and waited out a hail of bullets blasting into the locker's metal facade. A smoky haze filled the air from the gunfire. Heavy footfalls continued echoing from the stairwell, growing louder with each pounding foot.

They're not expecting me to run.

Danny sprinted for the stairwell. He held the AR at the ready, pulling the trigger when the first man appeared at the bottom landing. He collapsed before he could raise his pistol toward Danny.

Bullets flew past Danny's head from behind. The moment he entered the stairwell, a pistol whipped him across the cheek.

Danny's entire face grew numb, blood oozing down his chin. His assailant stood with his arm still extended, flashing an evil grin. He swung his pistol toward Danny's face again, this time with his finger on the trigger.

A third man came hurtling down the stairs and lost his footing as he rounded the above landing. He shouted while tumbling down the stairs, taking out his colleague like a bowling ball.

The man fired a shot, but it sailed past Danny's head and out the door into the warehouse.

Danny planted two rounds into each of their heads. Aside from his own panting breath, silence enveloped the warehouse. The others surely hadn't fled. Had they moved into hiding? Gone for reinforcements?

They mentioned Steele had been contacted. He might have called his men off, wanting to face Danny himself. When Danny stared back into the warehouse, he found it deserted. Perhaps they'd all seen enough.

Danny retreated into the warehouse and peered out the door. A car zoomed away from the building, leaving puffs of dust in its wake.

"Cowards."

When Danny turned around, more footsteps came from the stairwell. He tightened his grip on the AR and waited. A minute later, three people appeared in the stairwell doorway, all unarmed. Two men and a woman. All of Latin descent.

Danny's stomach lurched at the sight of them. They froze when they spotted Danny and his rifle.

"You!" Danny shouted. "You're the ones who kidnapped my mom."

The man on the left reached behind his waist. Danny shot him twice in the chest. The woman shrieked, slapping her hands over her mouth.

Danny charged toward the remaining two. "Where is she?! Tell me right now and I'll spare you."

The woman spoke first. "Sh-sh-she's on the fourth floor. Please don't hurt me!"

The man next to her held his hands up, freezing in place.

"Is she on the fourth floor?" Danny asked the man, who only nodded, eyes wide with shock.

These people aren't killers. Hired hands to do others' dirty work. Killers didn't have panic attacks with a gun pointed at them.

"Get the hell out of here and leave town," Danny said. "If I ever see either of you again, I promise to put a slug between your eyes."

They hesitated for a few seconds, taking cautious steps toward the exit. They didn't appear to believe Danny was actually letting them pass. But he did.

Once they were out of the building, Danny returned to the stairwell and climbed to the fourth floor.

Each floor had rooms lining the walls against the open hallways. Danny kicked open each door, finding the rooms empty. On the fourth one, however, he found his mother lying on a bed, belts strapped around her limbs to keep her tied down.

Her head turned toward him, and they made eye contact.

"Oh, Danny." Tears filled Tatiana's eyes, her voice weak enough that Danny almost didn't hear her. "I knew you'd come."

Tears welled in his own eyes. Seeing his mom strapped down like a rabid animal made him both sick and enraged. Knowing it was for a valid reason made the reality that much harder to see.

"Mom," he whispered.

Danny stepped all the way into the room, approaching his mother's bedside.

Her head rolled back and forth, eyes glazed over as they struggled to focus on her son. "Armando," she said. "Mi amor. I've missed you."

"I'm not Dad," Danny said, lowering himself to brush a hand over his mother's forehead. "I'm Danny. Mom, do you know who I am? Do you know who you are, or where you are?"

"Armando," Tatiana repeated, a smile touching her lips. "Mi amor."

"Dammit, Ma!" Danny cried. "Don't do this to me. Don't forget me."

Through bleary vision, Danny undid the belts tying his mother down. When he finished, he picked up her frail body and helped her into her wheelchair, steering her out toward the elevator.

"C'mon, Ma. Let's get you out of here."

CHAPTER THIRTY-FOUR

DANNY SPENT the next week in seclusion with his mother, not worried about Steele or Calloway finding him.

He found a campground near the Maryland-Pennsylvania border and paid for a month's stay in a cabin overlooking Prettyboy Reservoir. The campground didn't require a credit card and was happy to take Danny's cash. They didn't require an ID either, so he used a fake name to check in. The two of them settled in, comfortably off the grid.

Danny nursed his mother back to reasonable health, giving her meds at precisely the correct times. She experienced fewer outbursts, and after three days, Danny helped her out of bed to return to her wheelchair. The cabin had a ramp she used to go outside and soak in the surrounding nature.

Danny had traveled across the Pennsylvania border to place calls to Zak and Nadia. Zak never answered his phone after delivering his remarks to the press pool, but Nadia kept him in the loop.

They were also hiding in an undisclosed location—Nadia refused to share the details in case their calls were being monitored. She had taken another week off work and now faced disciplinary action upon her return. But she appeared unfazed by the threat.

"No, the time off wasn't planned," she had explained to Danny. "But I have the hours. If they fire me over this, we should have a fun day in court."

They had last spoken three days ago, with tentative plans to speak again tomorrow. Considering how they all needed to keep their phones off, scheduling their conversations in advance was the only safe approach.

Through it all, Danny declined to leave the area. Sure, he could've taken his mother and returned to Colorado—even with the hell a drive across the country would've proven to be with her. But Steele, Ellis, and Calloway all roamed freely. Still.

Marcus Vance remained in hiding, and he deserved a reunion with his family. Eva Ramirez couldn't have died for no good reason. Her sacrifice wasn't lost on Danny. His only regret was never thanking her for taking the bullet.

She had popped into his thoughts more than once since the news of her death had broken. Danny didn't understand *why* she had become so motivated to sacrifice herself. She could've approached everything differently and still been alive today, helping him figure out their next move.

But Danny kept the news on all day and night, waiting for word out of D.C. about formal charges against Senator Calloway.

It wasn't until their seventh day in the cabin that the news reported an upcoming special announcement live from the Senate. They broke to a commercial, promising to return with coverage.

"This is it, Ma!" Danny cried.

He had tried keeping her up to speed with everything going on to no avail. The story had too many unfamiliar names and faces for her to follow. After drawing diagrams of how all the people were connected to each other and to Calloway, Danny had given up. His mother would watch him watch the news and adapt her reactions based on his.

Danny sat in the lounge chair facing the TV with his mom settled in her wheelchair next to him.

"What's this coming on?" she asked. "No more political shows, I hope."

"Sorry, Ma. But remember what I said. If this goes well, we'll get to go home and return to our normal lives."

"Back to New Mexico?"

Danny's heart seized. "Colorado, Ma. You haven't lived in New Mexico since you were a teenager."

Danny had never forgotten what a doctor told him in the early days of his mom's diagnosis. *When her memories revert to childhood, the end is near.*

Her teenage years weren't quite childhood, but a move in that direction. Danny had spent enough time with his mother throughout his life to have heard stories from her youth. Once she started talking about the times she'd tagged along with her mother during her shifts at the small-town hospital, Danny would worry. Until then, he trusted she still had plenty of days left.

The news station returned from its commercial break, the anchors speaking over the live feed showing inside the senate.

"In just a few moments, Senator Whitehorse from New Mexico is expected to deliver his initial remarks after a special senate committee has been investigating the accusations against Senator Calloway of Louisiana."

"Whitehorse!" Danny shouted. "He's the one Eva took the documents to."

"Who's Eva?" his mom replied.

"Don't worry, Ma. I've got a good feeling about this."

And he did. Would people call it butterflies? That sensation of fluttering in his gut in anticipation of life-changing news? He hadn't experienced that feeling—at least, not positively—in many years. Hard to have butterflies when life was nothing more than death, rejection, and survival.

But if Calloway had charges pressed against him, how long would it take for this entire operation to crumble? Those who remained might try to keep things afloat, but doing so would be stupid. If they had Calloway on the ropes, their investigation would only lead deeper until they discovered everyone who helped him.

"We now shift our coverage to the Senate," the anchor said.

The volume changed as Senator Whitehorse stepped to a podium in front of his colleagues.

Whitehorse had served in the senate for the past ten years. A young man in his mid-thirties when he'd first entered, gray streaks now decorated his once black hair. To represent his Native American heritage, he wore an aqua-colored bolo tie over his suit. He spread out papers on the podium and folded his hands over them.

"Ladies and gentlemen of the Senate. My fellow Americans. Last week, heavy accusations were brought forth against one of our own, Senator Richard Calloway. The accusations came with supporting documentation about his involvement in a scheme involving the DEA and CIA."

The camera panned to Senator Calloway, sitting in his usual post among his peers. A smug expression plastered on his face, Danny's hopes were dashed. He didn't have the look of someone expecting upcoming charges.

"For the past week," Whitehorse continued, "I have been hard at work with a special committee of both Democrats and Republicans to investigate these accusations brought forth by trusted sources. I want to first thank those senators on the committee for their tireless work around the clock."

Whitehorse named all fifteen senators who had worked on the committee.

Why does it feel like he's stalling? Danny wondered. *You don't stall when you have good news.*

"Over this past week, we've conducted over fifty interviews with parties privy to the happenings of the aforementioned government departments. We reviewed thousands of pages of documents related to the accusations and have uncovered some disturbing truths.

"The first matter to address is Senator Calloway. As a reminder, the senator has not had formal charges pressed against him. This is not a trial. Our work was an exploratory investigation. While the senator has worked closely with others who are potentially involved with the accusations, we found no evidence of his involvement."

"WHAT?!" Danny jumped out of his chair, gawking at the TV.

"It is my distinct pleasure to announce Senator Calloway is an innocent man. He is free to continue his work for the United States and his constituents from the great state of Louisiana without the shadow of these accusations looming over his head."

"This can't be for real," Danny said. He paced around their living area, running circles around his mother, who only watched him for his first couple of laps.

"What is it, Danny?" she asked. "I don't understand."

What the hell is going on? Calloway has dirt on Whitehorse, too? This can't be happening.

"We're not going home anytime soon, Ma. Let me hear what he's saying."

Whitehorse continued. "While Senator Calloway's name has been cleared, our investigation has led us to others who have been involved with corrupt, illegal actions. Further investigations will be required to complete a list of those involved.

"As of now, Deputy Administrator Charles Steele of the DEA has been found to have heavy involvement with an international crime ring. We have presented our findings to a federal judge and have received a warrant for Mr. Steele's arrest. We will also share our findings with the House of Representatives with a recommendation for the impeachment of Mr. Steele."

Danny rubbed his forehead. Each word coming out of Whitehorse's mouth added to the messy layers of emotions swarming his mind.

They're using Steele as the scapegoat now? At least he's getting what he *deserves, but this only makes it harder to pin anything on Calloway.*

"Is this bad, Danny?" his mom asked.

Danny gazed at the TV. Whitehorse concluded his remarks, and the anchors returned to the feed briefly, before an image of Steele replaced them.

In just five minutes, Whitehorse shifted the entire focus away from Calloway and onto Steele.

"Calloway had to have done something for this to happen," Danny said. "Impossible they found nothing tied to him."

"Don't you work at the DEA, Danny?" his mom asked. She was trying her best to follow this story. Danny couldn't fault her for that.

"Not anymore, Ma. And maybe it's for the best. But I still know somebody who does."

CHAPTER THIRTY-FIVE

A WITCH HUNT broke out over the next two hours, and Danny enjoyed every moment from the television coverage.

Once the reality settled in that Tatiana would have to stay in the cabin, she promptly consoled Danny and assured him of her comfort in the new place.

"I actually always wanted to live somewhere like this," she had told him while brushing his cheek with her thin fingers. "But I never could afford it."

Thirty minutes after Senator Whitehorse delivered his remarks, federal authorities claimed Steele to be armed and dangerous. A Washington police officer explained their involvement in searching for Steele and warned anyone who might see him to stand back and call the police.

After that, the news covered the breaking story of the nation's DEA administrator on the run from authorities. Police searched Steele's house. His office. His mother's house. He was nowhere to be found.

Danny imagined his nemesis hiding and panicking.

Hope he's enjoying the dose of his own medicine.

It wasn't reported, but Danny believed the government would've invalidated Steele's passport, preventing him from leaving the country. Nowhere to run. Plenty of places to hide.

Chaos had flipped D.C. upside down. Congressional representatives went on TV to shout accusations against their colleagues. Others fired back. Social media became flooded with even more hostility and false statements about Calloway and Steele.

This nationwide search for Steele wouldn't have received so much coverage unless those releasing the statements understood the truth about Steele.

Just moments earlier, Senator Whitehorse had merely mentioned Steele's name. Now, he had become the most sought-after man in the country.

Danny's mom had dozed off, the news no longer holding her interest. He guided her to bed and returned to the TV for the remainder of the afternoon. At five o'clock, Danny fed his mother dinner, bathed her, and got her ready for bed, where she watched old reruns of sitcoms until falling asleep.

She lay peacefully, her chest rising and falling with each breath. Despite having just been kidnapped and held hostage, Danny couldn't deny the instant tranquility this cabin provided for both of them.

Danny trusted he could venture away from the cabin for a few moments. He took a ten-minute drive across the Pennsylvania border and parked in a gas station parking lot.

Even though they hadn't made plans to speak until the next day, Danny dialed Nadia.

"Danny!" she answered after one ring.

"Thank God you picked up. I take it you've seen the news?"

"I've been following every update I can find."

"Just you?"

"Yeah ... Zak turned his phone back on when the news broke. And sure enough, he received a call from the Attorney General." Her tone became serious. "They asked him to return to headquarters and take over as the acting administrator until this gets resolved."

Danny's gut twisted. This would put an even larger target on his friend's back. "Zak's in D.C. already?"

"Yes, we're back. He received the call about fifteen minutes after Whitehorse's speech and headed straight in." Nadia exhaled a heavy breath. "Danny, this is all good, right?"

Danny took a moment to ponder the question. It wasn't a simple yes or no.

"Steele's been exposed, which should help those of us he blackmailed. But they never mentioned anything about Ellis." Danny rubbed his neck, allowing his train of thought to become verbal. How does the head of the CIA remain untouched after all this? "Steele was definitely running the logistics of this operation, but Ellis was pulling the strings. I saw tons of emails between him and Calloway. That guy is one of the most connected people in Washington. Who knows what else he's been lying about? I'm sure if they barge into the CIA right now, Ellis will act like he has no idea what's going on."

"And people will believe him."

"Of course they will. And why not? It's not like the DEA and CIA have ever had much overlap in their work. Their collaboration was a new initiative brought on by Steele. And Ellis will point to that very fact, especially now that Steele is their fall guy."

"And Calloway?" Nadia asked.

"Even more powerful than Ellis. Calloway might be the most dangerous person in Washington. He's pulling all of the strings. No way in hell he walks free unless he threatened Whitehorse with something. He's been a senator for what, twenty-five years? He knows everyone's dark secrets. That's how these guys rise to power so easily. They threaten each other to get what they want, then all go out to dinner and pretend like they're best friends."

Nadia was silent for a moment. Danny imagined her pacing the room, as she always did while on a phone call. "What are we supposed to do now?"

"You've done enough, Nadia. You should get on a plane and go home. Save your job. Don't burn that bridge, especially if you plan to come back to Washington. You'll need that reference."

"I've thought about it," she said, "but I can't just leave. Not now. I'm glad your mom's safe, but it seems cowardly to flee town. Even if I have nothing else to offer here."

"That's your choice to make. Who knows how long it will take until we can travel around the city safely?" Danny squeezed his phone, frustrated his life was being dictated by mad men. "How did Zak seem? Think he'll answer if I call?"

"He seemed…emboldened, I'd say. Confident. Like a switch flipped and he no longer has to worry about being caught. Can't say what all he's dealing with, but I'm sure he'd prioritize your call if possible."

"He should storm into that office with all the confidence in the world," Danny said. "We know his name isn't showing up on any documents they're investigating. He may be the only one in that department who didn't sell his soul for a few dollars."

"Call him then. I'm sure you two have plenty to discuss."

"I will. And Nadia? Thanks for coming out here. You didn't have to. You could've gone home that night, told yourself everything was fine, and that you weren't really being followed. I can't imagine what would've happened if you did that. Thanks for trusting me."

Nadia sighed. "Oh, Danny. We may have a complicated relationship, but I'll always trust you. Funny enough, trust is the least of our problems. But we can discuss all this later. There's a criminal on the run, and you and Zak need to find him."

Danny chuckled. She always could read his mind. "Bye, Nadia. Talk soon."

He hung up and gathered his thoughts. Nadia always threw a wrench into his emotions. Just when he thought he'd put her in the back of his thoughts—the back of his heart—she came crawling back.

Danny shook his head clear of Nadia and dialed Zak's burner phone.

It rang only twice before he answered. "Dan, I don't have much time. You talk to Nadia?"

"I did. Congrats on the promotion. About damn time."

"Wish it felt more like a celebration."

"We'll celebrate when this is all finished. What's going on over there?"

"First off, I cleared your name. Ellis had agents hunting you down. I have some connections with influence in that agency, and convinced them to call off the search. Otherwise, our federal government is running around like chickens with their heads cut off. Seriously, I feel like I'm the only one thinking logically right now. Staying calm."

"That's why you're in the role," Danny said. "As you should have been before now."

"We've been raiding Steele's office. Turning out every file he's kept. Going through his computer." Zak hesitated a moment, the background filled with light chatter. "He left a note."

Danny's stomach roiled. "What's it say?"

"Probably not supposed to share it, but what the hell. This place is basically anarchy now."

"Don't get fired on your first day."

"To whom it may concern, please accept this letter as my formal resignation from the post of administrator for the Drug Enforcement Administration. It is my great regret to step down from this role, as I've spent my entire adult life dedicated to the mission of the DEA.

"I apologize to anyone I hurt through my actions. I leave this post a humbled man. Greed got the best of me, as it has many men throughout our nation's history. I got in too deep and never realized the harm I caused. I don't expect forgiveness but maybe understanding. Time is too precious to waste by listing all my justifications for doing what I did. Just know that harming innocent people was never in my plans.

"Trust in our institutions has been damaged, and I accept my responsibility for that. I also believe everything will return to normal in due time. I wish nothing but the best for the DEA and the United States. God bless. Charles Lester Steele."

"Wow," Danny said. "A resignation *and* confession all in the same letter?"

"Don't read too much into the confession part." Disgust dripped from each word Zak said. "You and I know what he's referring to, but it'll never hold up in a trial. He never mentioned what he actually did. All empty words to make him look better. Maybe cleanse his own soul."

He's gonna need a cleansed soul where he's headed. Prick.

"What's the next move, then?"

"Our next twelve hours are entirely focused on finding him," Zak said. "We're going through his files for clues. But there are over two hundred locations mentioned. We're dealing with a needle in a haystack. I've eliminated all locations like hotels. He's not going to hide somewhere with that much foot traffic. It'll be somewhere off the grid. Remote. Likely somewhere we'd never think of searching."

A grin touched Danny's lips. "I know where he is."

CHAPTER THIRTY-SIX

BY THE LOOKS OF IT, Steele's support had slipped since the news broke. Last time, about a dozen vehicles were parked outside the warehouse. Tonight, only three awaited when Danny drove in, the AR-15 riding in the passenger seat.

He had no proof Steele was inside, but this was the safest place for him to hide after leaving his duties at the DEA.

Danny's current plan was to barge into the building and open fire. Spray bullets in every direction. Anyone remaining loyal to Steele at this point in time was fully committed. There would be no negotiating or reasoning with any of them.

I'll kill everyone inside, Danny thought.

But those who had remained loyal to Steele were ready.

The moment Danny stepped out of his truck, AR cocked and ready, guns fired from the only row of windows in the warehouse. His windshield exploded into hundreds of shards. Danny dropped and rolled toward the back of the truck.

They had maybe an hour of sunlight remaining in the day. Danny had no interest in letting this shootout continue past sunset. He checked the roof for any hidden shooters, found none, and jumped out from behind his truck.

The guns shot in unison. Danny pinpointed where the gunmen were positioned in the windows. Two of them, judging by the flashes from their muzzles. He dove back behind the truck, his focus kicking into high gear.

Time slowed down as he plotted his next moves. He hadn't played competitive sports since his high school days, but he found himself ready to juke, spin, and fake out his attackers.

Danny ran three steps from the truck, pivoted, then jumped back behind it. The gunshots were delayed, landing in the gravel seconds after he had stood there. Having anticipated that, Danny lunged back out and fired ten rapid shots toward the first shooter.

More rounds showered upon Danny's truck as he hid behind the bed again.

I can't sit out here forever. How long until they send someone to force me out from behind the truck?

Danny tested the waters first. He stepped to the same area now littered with spent rounds. The gunshots were even more delayed. But Danny spotted only one flash from the window.

No way I killed the first guy from this far out.

Danny stood seventy-five feet from the building. Sure, he could've hit a target if given enough time to line up a shot. But firing blindly into the distance?

He had no more time to waste. He jumped from the truck, opening fire at the other window while sprinting toward the building's entrance.

The shooter responded with a flurry of gunfire. But Danny charged forward, gravel and dirt exploding all around him from the errant shots. A man with a shotgun stepped into the doorway, gun aimed at Danny.

Danny slid like a baseball player stealing second base, swinging the AR downward and squeezing the trigger five more times until the man in the door fell backward.

He jolted to his feet and stepped inside the warehouse, relieved to be out of range of the shooter in the window above. Four men were spread across the warehouse, guns fixed on Danny. When no one pulled the trigger, Danny did. He mowed them down left to right. One of their returned shots caught Danny in his left biceps, the wound burning like fire.

He gritted his teeth, relying on the adrenaline and shock to numb the pain while he hunted down Steele.

The four men who had greeted him inside all lay dead across the warehouse floor, blood pooling around their bodies. Danny checked the growing moisture inside his left sleeve. The wound bled, but not enough to warrant a self-made tourniquet.

"Come out and fight me like a man, Steele!" Danny shouted. His words echoed around the warehouse, falling on only his ears. "Anyone else in here working for you? Come out, you cowards!"

Danny refused to step deeper into the warehouse. From his position in the doorway, the pathways of the other floors inside—visible from the main level—were just out of sight. There could have been fifty others with guns waiting up there for Danny to take a step into the middle of the floor. Instant firing squad.

A loud crackling sounded from further in. An intercom speaker.

"Danny Cortez." Steele's voice carried from the speaker and bounced around the deserted warehouse. "Half the federal government is looking for me, and yet here you are. Don't you have a mother you should be nursing back to health? You just can't leave me alone, can you? It seems we're destined to do this dance until one of us calls it quits."

"Come out here, Steele!" Danny scanned the warehouse back and forth, checking the stairwell door every few seconds. He thought of his mother left on her own. She was still able to feed herself, especially with the easy setup Danny left her with. But he needed to get back to her. Soon.

Steele laughed through the intercom. "I welcome you to my humble abode. By the way, kudos to you for breaking your mom out of here. I truly underestimated you. Who would've thought an old intelligence analyst had more guts and skills than anyone else working in the field? You were in the wrong job, my friend."

He's trying to sweet talk me into lowering my guard.

"You're done, Steele. Authorities are already on their way. Why don't you come out and turn yourself in with whatever dignity you have left?"

Steele laughed again, a sound that became more maniacal with each passing moment. "I'm curious, Cortez. What are you getting out of this? You're not even employed by the government anymore. You're out here bringing down a criminal operation as a hobby? Make it make sense."

"I'm making the world a better place," Danny shouted. "Enough of the powerful becoming more powerful. You people have no end to your greed or lust for control. All it does is hurt everyone else. You let criminals walk free for their compliance. That's not a world I want to live in. So, I had to take matters into my own hands."

"Ahh, so noble of you, Cortez. Our own little hero. Have you ever stopped to think how useless your efforts are? Sure, you may win this battle, but this is bigger than both of us. If I go down today, things might calm down for a bit. But it will all come back. This isn't the first major scandal in Washington, and it won't be the last."

Steele's words weighed on Danny. Despite all his efforts, Steele was right. How did Danny's fight against this corruption fit into the bigger picture? Senator Calloway was deemed an innocent man. And he wouldn't stop his operation just because Steele got caught. No, he'd adjust. Adapt. Get even better at evading the authorities and accountability.

The thought made Danny sick. But he was beyond the point of leaving the warehouse. He had come here to see this through. For his mother. For Zak. And Nadia. What would they think if Danny simply returned home now?

"You're done, Steele. You can wait this out, or I can come find you. What's it going to be?"

"Oh, Danny Boy, how wrong you are. See, you're in my house now. And we play by my rules. I'd like to have a word with you. In person. No guns. No weapons. What do you say?"

The shadow from the doorway was subtle, but Danny caught it from the corner of his eye.

Too late, however.

He whipped his AR around, but a man dressed in full tactical gear was already on him. The man also held a rifle. Instead of shooting Danny, he whipped him across the head with the barrel.

Danny collapsed to the ground, swallowed by blackness.

CHAPTER THIRTY-SEVEN

DANNY AWOKE WITH A POUNDING HEADACHE.

Handcuffs fastened his wrists to the legs of a wooden chair, pulling his body into an awkward, hunchbacked position.

He raised his head, his gaze zooming in and out of focus as it settled on Steele leaning against a wall with his arms crossed.

They were in an empty room. The only door remained closed. Aside from the chair Danny was strapped to, the only other object was another man standing in the corner, sunglasses concealing his eyes.

"Good morning, sunshine." Steele approached Danny but kept fifteen feet between them. "Have a nice nap?"

Danny's head throbbed like a nail had been jammed through its center. "Where are we?"

Steele grinned. "Still in the same warehouse. Just thought we'd be more cozy in this room." He glanced around at the empty walls. "Not a bad place to die, wouldn't you say?"

"I always thought your coffin would be much smaller. But whatever floats your boat."

Steele howled with laughter. "Oh, Cortez, I'm gonna miss that sense of humor. It really is too bad things didn't work out differently. If you'd played your cards differently, you'd probably be a multimillionaire by now. Living the best life. Instead, you get to die in an abandoned warehouse in this dump of a city."

Danny hadn't told Zak where he was going. He'd preferred to confirm Steele's whereabouts first before having Zak pull resources. But he'd left his cellphone and the GPS turned on.

Someone would eventually show up, and it didn't matter who. Danny just needed someone else to buy him some time.

"And here *you* are," Danny said. "Still chasing all the money in the world like it can fill that void in your miserable soul. Haven't you learned by now, Steele? This money has turned you into a terrible person. You can be as rich as you'd like, but there's still no one who loves you."

As Danny made subtle movements in the chair, its creaking noises suggested its vulnerability.

Just knock me over already.

But Steele only grinned in response to Danny's harsh words.

A frantic pounding banged on the door. Steele's grin vanished as he turned. The man in the corner jumped into action and pulled open the door.

It was another of Steele's goons, only this one wasn't coward enough to hide his face. The man had a thick beard in need of grooming. He panted for air, placing his hands on his knees.

"What is it?" Steele demanded.

The man stood tall, horror in his eyes. "Calloway, sir."

"What about Calloway?"

"He's here. We tried telling him he couldn't enter, but he pushed through. Has lots of guys with him. Maybe fifteen. We couldn't stop them. Weren't even sure if we were supposed to."

Steele's mouth hung open. "Did he say what he wants?"

The man shook his head. "Refused to tell us. He's on his way up here."

Up here. So we're on a higher floor.

Steele pulled out his cell phone. "I don't see any missed calls. Why didn't he call me? What's going on?"

Both of Steele's goons exchanged glances and shrugged. Whatever had been planned here had clearly gone off course.

The sound of heavy marching came from the hallway outside the door. At least a dozen different pairs of footsteps clopped along, getting closer.

"What the hell?" Steele said, taking a step back from the door.

Men and women dressed in black suits, like the secret service, stepped into the room first. Five of them. They glanced around, eyed Danny, and the one nearest the door said, "All clear!"

Three seconds later, Senator Richard Calloway strolled into the room. "What the hell is this, Steele?" His southern drawl sounded even thicker in person. "I'm sure you're in a panic, but now you've got a man tied to a chair. Let him go. Now!"

"Senator Calloway." Steele's voice wavered, fear creeping in. "Why are you here, sir?"

"Why am I here? Son, why are *you* here? I thought you'd be sneaking across the Canadian border by now. But you're still playing these silly games. What have I told you since the beginning? We're not the mob. Not the mafia. Or those cartels you hunt down."

Steele hung his head, clearly ashamed. "Correct, sir."

"Then why the hell are you acting like a mob boss? What're you going to do to this man? Cut his fingers off and put them in a jar?"

"Sir, this is Danny—"

"I don't give a rat's ass who that is. If you have any interest in your future, you need to let him go right now. Clear?"

"Yes, sir." Steele cowered like a punished child, looking to his men for help, but getting nothing in return. "Sir, if you'll just let me explain—"

"You've said enough. Shut the hell up and listen to me. I turned you in, son. Hate to say it, but I didn't like where that investigation was headed. I had to make a move before they caught me."

Steele's voice no longer held fear, only rage. "So you threw me under the bus?"

"Just for now, Steele. Dammit. Shut up and listen, I said. You'll spend a few months in a cushy federal jail awaiting your trial. You might even get sentenced to prison. But I'll get you a presidential pardon. This is a federal case, anyway, so you've nothing else to worry about. Give me a year or two to get that pardon, and you'll be a free man. Assuming you don't kidnap and murder this guy and add to your charges. We'll reward you handsomely for your sacrifice."

"If it's so easy," Steele said, his gaze growing wicked, "why don't you turn yourself in?".

Calloway chuckled. "I can't do much from inside a jail cell. If I go down, it's only a matter of time before everyone else does. Keep me innocent and on the outside, and I can make things happen. Speaking of, someone slipped Whitehorse some very damning documents. Had to make some big concessions for New Mexico to get him to drop those —not that they would've held up in court as valid evidence. But still. I make problems go away, you see. Now, free this man and face your destiny, Steele."

Calloway glanced at Danny, the two locking eyes. The senator spoke in a harsh tone. "You say a word about anything you heard in here and we'll find you. Stick a shotgun where the sun don't shine, squeeze that trigger and feed you to the gators. You hear me, son?"

Danny nodded, his throat locked with tension. *Is he actually going to let me live? Was it only Steele who wanted me dead?*

Steele let out an inhuman growl as he reached inside his suit jacket. He whipped out a pistol and aimed it at Senator Calloway.

Three guns fired in unison.

Charles Steele dropped to the floor, flat on his back. Blood oozed from his chest, while more poured out of his mouth. His head landed about ten feet away from Danny, eyes glaring at the ceiling, a moan issuing from his lips.

Calloway shook his head. "Such a stupid man. Leave him here. Tell the cops he tried to shoot me, and my team responded. And get this man uncuffed and out of there, for Christ's sake. Let's go."

One of Calloway's men strolled over to Danny and slipped a key into the handcuffs. "You heard the senator. Go home. Speak nothing of this."

Danny rolled his wrists, which had gone numb. "You got it. One last word with Steele?"

The man nodded and strode toward the door, stepping over Steele's limp body.

Danny stood over Steele, whose stare found him. The slightest of grins touched his lips.

"Something funny, Chuck?" Danny asked. "Sounds like you've had plenty of warnings to avoid this situation. I guess you really had no control over your greed after all."

Steele struggled to get the words out through the gurgles of blood. "You're…dead."

"I'm dead? That's not how it looks to me. See, I'm going to leave here and go home. Might cook a nice steak dinner for me and my ma to celebrate. Hell, might even stop and buy a cigar on my way home. Life is feeling that great right now. I never have to see you again. The DEA is back in good hands with Zak, just as it should be. I'd say it was nice knowing you, but that would be a lie."

Steele swallowed three times in succession, flashing a bloody smile. "You think this ends…with me? Calloway knew…who you were. Didn't want to make a…scene. He'll be back. You're just a pawn, too… Cortez. Wait and see."

Steele stopped shivering, and his eyes glossed over. Danny stepped over his body and exited the warehouse, sirens approaching in the distance.

CHAPTER THIRTY-EIGHT

DANNY WOKE the next morning in the safety of his cabin to the tune of songbirds outside his window. The heavy comforter weighed down on his exhausted body, living up to its name.

When he had returned home the night before, his mother snoozed peacefully, oblivious to the hell her son had just endured.

Despite the unbearable fatigue, Danny had struggled to fall asleep. Steele's last words weighed on his mind. His old nemesis had raised valid points. Calloway had to have known who Danny was. If he was running the entire operation, he'd surely been briefed about all potential threats, such as Danny Cortez.

Would Calloway really allow Danny to live his life in peace? He doubted it but held on to hope.

He had fallen asleep shortly after midnight and woken at seven o'clock, his mother calling his name from the other room.

Danny found his mom sitting up in bed with a welcoming grin. "Good morning, Ma. You ready for breakfast? I can make us some eggs and bacon."

"Bacon? You never have to ask me twice."

Danny laughed and headed for the kitchen, finding his cell phone on the counter. He forgot he had called Nadia last night, his throbbing mind in a daze, and told her to come over this morning.

She texted him around six-thirty, informing him she was on her way with Zak. On cue, a knock rapped on the door.

"Who's there?" his mom shouted from her room.

"Nadia and Zak, Ma. Nothing to worry about."

Just hearing those words come out of his mouth sent a wave of relief through Danny. He couldn't recall the last time he had nothing to worry about. Lounging around a cabin on whatever day of the week it was, making breakfast for his mom to enjoy with a view of the lake outside? Perfection.

Danny peeked through the window next to the door, confirmed his friends stood outside, and pulled it open.

Nadia lunged in and threw her arms around Danny. "I'm so glad you're safe. I was watching the news about that warehouse all night. Steele's really dead?"

She pulled away as tears welled in her eyes.

"He is," Danny said.

Zak stepped forward and hugged his friend, clapping him on the back. "Good work, Dan. You could have let me handle it. I had guys ready to go anywhere I said."

Danny nodded. "I know. But I needed to make sure he was actually there. Things worked themselves out. Did the news mention Calloway was at the warehouse?"

"Calloway was *at* the warehouse?" Nadia asked. "No. The news said Steele tried to shoot Calloway somewhere in D.C. before fleeing to the warehouse. They never said where, though."

Danny laughed. "Wow. That guy has just about everyone in town paid off. He was there. Came to tell Steele he turned him in. Steele flipped out and pulled a gun on Calloway. His guards shot and killed Steele."

"You saw all this?" Zak asked.

Danny nodded. "Steele was going to kill me. Tied me to a chair. Calloway showing up saved my life. I suppose I owe him that much."

"You don't owe him a damn thing," Zak said, his tone laced with disgust. "I'm in a position of authority now. Calloway can't buy me off."

Danny delivered a playful punch to Zak's shoulder. "Look at you embracing your role like you were meant for it."

Zak grinned. "It's early. But word around the office is once my name is officially cleared of any involvement with Steele, the president plans to nominate me for administrator."

"What?" Nadia slapped Zak on his other arm. "You didn't tell me that."

"I wanted to share the news with both of you."

"We have to get you a new suit," Danny said. "You have a Senate confirmation hearing coming up."

Zak smiled. "I can't believe everything that's happened. But for it to all end this way for me…I'm shocked. None of it feels real yet."

"Well, you've earned it, my friend. I couldn't be prouder of you."

"Danny?" his mother called out.

Nadia sprang into action. "I'll go. Haven't seen her in a while!"

She rushed into the bedroom, leaving Danny alone with Zak. They moved to stand around the kitchen, everyone apparently too excited to sit down.

He turned to his friend. "So, what's going on in the office?"

"Pure chaos. That's why we came so early—hope you don't mind. I have to head in by nine. Will probably be there through the night." Zak shook his head. "We're working with auditors reviewing all electronic and physical files that have touched Steele during his entire tenure with the DEA. My understanding is that something similar is happening at the CIA, but no word has come out about guilty parties. Yet."

"You think they'll bust Ellis?"

Zak shrugged. "Hearing about Calloway and how *he's* getting away with everything, who knows."

"Do you plan to build a case against Calloway?"

"I'd like to. Won't be something I do right away. Want to see what comes out of all this auditing first. Maybe they'll find something tied back to him. I'm not counting on it, but a man can dream. My first order of business is restoring trust in the DEA. No one is thinking fondly of our department right now."

"You're just the man for the job."

"I hope you're right, Dan. My work is cut out for me. Long uphill battle for the next year, at least. Anyone caught having aided Steele with any of his shady dealings will be fired. We're gonna have a ton of hiring to fill those roles, and stricter vetting processes to follow. Steele might be gone, but his damage is going to linger for a while."

"I'm sorry to hear that, man. Let me know if I can help in any way."

The corner of Zak's mouth lifted. "You want your old job back? Or maybe a promotion?"

Danny thought back to his life working in the DEA. He'd loved it. Until he didn't. He grinned, drumming his fingers on the chair in front of him. "You'd love that. But no thanks."

"What's next for Danny Cortez then?"

"Later this morning, I get to call Marcus Vance and tell him he's free to go home. I was worried I'd never get to make that call. Glad it gets to happen now. His family has been through hell with this secret. Beyond that, I have nothing planned. I'll probably stay here with Ma as long as she'd like. I'm afraid she doesn't have much time left. This place is peaceful, and if she wants to, I'll stay with her until the end."

Zak pursed his lips and stared at the floor. "I'm sorry, Dan. Take all the time you need. Cherish these final days with her."

Nadia rolled Tatiana out of her bedroom in her wheelchair. "Your mom said you were supposed to be making breakfast."

Danny clapped his head. "Sorry, Ma. Let me start."

Zak raised a hand. "Let me and Nadia make breakfast. Why don't you two go hang out on the patio and watch the sunrise over the lake? It's a beautiful morning."

Danny's chest tightened at the suggestion. He'd never find a better friend than Zak.

He took his mother outside and parked her next to the open patio chair where he sat.

Tatiana reached over and grabbed her son's hand. "I'm proud of you, Danny."

"Proud of what, Ma?"

"Just you. Life hasn't been easy for either of us. But you've always moved forward. You remind me so much of your father. He'd be so incredibly proud of you."

"Thank you, Ma. I'm proud of you, too. Without you, I wouldn't be where I am."

They held hands and sat in silence for the next thirty minutes, enjoying the view of nature from their back step.

Danny had no issues spending the next few months in this cabin. The peace of the surrounding woods was all he needed to unwind from the hell that had consumed the last year of his life.

Nadia and Zak came out to join them, trays full of eggs, bacon, sausage, toast, and a canteen of orange juice.

"Breakfast is served," Nadia said, serving the first plate to Tatiana.

They all settled in their seats and devoured the breakfast.

"Thank you both for coming here," Danny said to his friends. "I didn't know how much I needed to see you after all that."

He locked eyes with Nadia. A familiar tension crackled between them. If she returned to D.C. for work, he wasn't sure he could resist. But that decision waited in the future. For now, Danny's only priority was keeping his mother as comfortable as possible.

"We're always here for you, Dan," Zak said. "You're never alone."

"With a view like this, all I need is an invitation," Nadia said.

"It is breathtaking."

They watched the lake. Fish jumped out of the water, rippling the surface. Ducks glided in and landed, ducklings following their mothers. And far across the way, a couple of boats sat in the middle, fishing poles dangling above the water.

Danny's phone buzzed with a text message. He pulled it out, curious since anyone he'd need to communicate with was right next to him.

Three words from a restricted number made him freeze.

CALLOWAY NEVER FORGETS.

Danny clenched his jaw and considered those gathered around him. His family. They all remained mesmerized by their view of the lake.

Not today.

He held his thumb down on the screen and deleted the text message.

The Story continues in Book 3 of
the Danny Cortez series: Widow Protocol.
Purchase your copy on Amazon!

Not ready to say goodbye? Grab a free Danny Cortez Prequel by signing up for newsletter at
https://liquidmind.media/danny-cortez-newsletter-signup-1/

THE DANNY CORTEZ SERIES

Dead Man's List
Shadow Directive
Widow Protocol

ALSO BY L.T. RYAN

Find All of L.T. Ryan's Books on Amazon Today!

The Jack Noble Series

The Recruit (free)

The First Deception (Prequel 1)

Noble Beginnings

A Deadly Distance

Ripple Effect (Bear Logan)

Thin Line

Noble Intentions

When Dead in Greece

Noble Retribution

Noble Betrayal

Never Go Home

Beyond Betrayal (Clarissa Abbot)

Noble Judgment

Never Cry Mercy

Deadline

End Game

Noble Ultimatum

Noble Legend

Noble Revenge

Never Look Back

The Devil's Bargain

Bear Logan Series

Ripple Effect

Blowback

Take Down

Deep State

Bear & Mandy Logan Series

Close to Home

Under the Surface

The Last Stop

Over the Edge

Between the Lies

Caught in the Web

The Marked Daughter

Beneath the Frozen Sky

What the Fog Hides

Rachel Hatch Series

Drift

Downburst

Fever Burn

Smoke Signal

Firewalk

Whitewater

Aftershock

Whirlwind

Tsunami

Fastrope

Sidewinder

Redaction

Mirage

Faultline

Switchback

Mitch Tanner Series

The Depth of Darkness

Into The Darkness

Deliver Us From Darkness

Cassie Quinn Series

Path of Bones

Whisper of Bones

Symphony of Bones

Etched in Shadow

Concealed in Shadow

Betrayed in Shadow

Born from Ashes

Return to Ashes

Risen from Ashes

Into the Light

Blake Brier Series

Unmasked

Unleashed

Uncharted

Drawpoint

Contrail

Detachment

Clear

Quarry

Dalton Savage Series

Savage Grounds

Scorched Earth

Cold Sky

The Frost Killer

Crimson Moon

Dust Devil

Savage Season

Maddie Castle Series

The Handler

Tracking Justice

Hunting Grounds

Vanished Trails

Smoldering Lies

Field of Bones

Beneath the Grove

Disappearing Act

Silent Witness

Affliction Z Series

Affliction Z: Patient Zero

Affliction Z: Abandoned Hope

Affliction Z: Descended in Blood

Affliction Z : Fractured Part 1

Affliction Z: Severed

Affliction Z: Dead Reckoning

Alex Hayes Series

Trial By Fire (Prequel)

Fractured Verdict

11th Hour Witness

Buried Testimony

The Bishop's Recusal

The Silent Gavel

Improper Influence

Stella LaRosa Series

Black Rose

Red Ink

Black Gold

White Lies

Silver Bullet

Avril Dahl Series

Cold Reckoning

Cold Legacy

Cold Mercy

Savannah Shadows Series

Echoes of Guilt

The Silence Before

Dead Air

Danny Cortez Series

Dead Man's List

Shadow Directive

Widow Protocol

Receive a free copy of The Recruit. Visit:

https://ltryan.com/jack-noble-newsletter-signup-1

ABOUT THE AUTHORS

L.T. RYAN is a *Wall Street Journal* and *USA Today* bestselling author, renowned for crafting pulse-pounding thrillers that keep readers on the edge of their seats. Known for creating gripping, character-driven stories, Ryan is the author of the *Jack Noble* series, the *Rachel Hatch* series, and more. With a knack for blending action, intrigue, and emotional depth, Ryan's books have captivated millions of fans worldwide.

Whether it's the shadowy world of covert operatives or the relentless pursuit of justice, Ryan's stories feature unforgettable characters and high-stakes plots that resonate with fans of Lee Child, Robert Ludlum, and Michael Connelly.

When not writing, Ryan enjoys crafting new ideas with coauthors, running a thriving publishing company, and connecting with readers. Discover the next story that will keep you turning pages late into the night.

Connect with L.T. Ryan
Sign up for his newsletter to hear the latest goings on and receive some free content
→ https://ltryan.com/jack-noble-newsletter-signup-1

Join the private readers' group
→ https://www.facebook.com/groups/1727449564174357

Instagram → @ltryanauthor

Visit the website → https://ltryan.com
Send an email → contact@ltryan.com

ANDRE GONZALEZ Andre Gonzalez is the international bestselling author of the Wealth of Time Series, and co-owner of M4L Publishing.

After surviving the Aurora Theater Shooting in 2012, Andre was inspired to chase his lifelong dream of pursuing a career as an author. This tragedy gave him a new appreciation for life along with a drive to make the world a better place by publishing books readers all around the world can enjoy.
He has written over twenty time-travel, thriller, and horror books after spending many years reading and studying the works of Stephen King and Dean Koontz. Keeping readers up late and their hearts pumping faster than normal is his ultimate goal. Andre was the recipient of the Rocky Mountain Fiction Writers 2021 Independent Writer of the Year award.

When he's not writing, you can find Andre buried underneath a long to-do list or chasing around his three hyper children. He and his wife are raising their family in their hometown of Denver, CO.

Connect with Andre:

Newsletter - https://andregonzalez.net/join-newsletter/
FB Group - https://www.facebook.com/groups/andregonzalezreaders
FB Page - https://www.facebook.com/AndreGonzalezAuthor
IG - www.instagram.com/monito0408

Made in United States
Orlando, FL
14 April 2026